LONG
Short Stories

Storybook 5 by TS Caladan

Long Short Stories – Storybook 5
Copyright © 2025 by TS Caladan

Edited by TS Caladan

Cover Art Design by TS Caladan

Published by TWB Press, https://www.twbpress.com

ISBN: 978-1-967888-01-6

<u>The Stories:</u>

1
Phantom of the Broadway Show

In 1968, Amandiss Hollington was not only the top Broadway critic in New York, he also wrote and produced stage plays. That fact appeared to be in opposition, yet Hollington's criticism of his own off-Broadway shows were extremely fair. He often blasted the "bad" performances of his actors and his choices he made in casting. Reviews of plays he'd written were reviewed by competing critics. His comments were discussed more than any other reviewer. The NY public, through newspapers, believed Amandiss Hollington was a quality producer and one of the best playwrights in town. Stage actors wanted to appear in his productions to further their careers and attach their names to his. Yet, his shows were not massive hits and were frequently *panned* or harshly described by his competition! Hollington needed a hit. He needed the *next big thing* so that his show would headline Broadway and pack the place, instead of a short off-Broadway run with small audiences and little profit.

Rumors had spread about this secluded "man of mystery" because of the insulated life he lived. He had no close friends. No intimate relationships. His photographs were always seen in the Variety and Entertainment Sections of the Times. People wanted to know who this man was and what made him tick. He wouldn't be interviewed. What was known about Hollington came from business associates who *hated him!* Amandiss was called: "cut-throat," "hateful," "back-stabber," "cold-blooded thief" and "a man you should not let near your daughter." The quotes were from people who knew of him and dealt with him, not from the general public. They somewhat adored him and his work.

Hollington had long, black hair and was thin. He wore thick, bulky sweaters, mostly. He was a coke addict, which explained his lifestyle. He lived alone in a 3-story brownstone that overlooked Central Park. His servant was named James. He cleaned and cooked for the playwright, but did not live on the premises.

After Amandiss snorted a fat line of cocaine, he

heard James, who said: "Sir, I brought your mail in earlier, but only now found this manilla folder on the doorstep. Addressed to you. No return address."

"Let's see that." Hollington grabbed the thick folder and said, "You may go, James." The short, bald man left the room.

He opened it and it was a new play that a man named Paul Polk wrote. Its title was: 'Dogs.'

"Ha, ha," Hollington laughed. *"Amusing.* Uh, ha. Ah. What's funny is some dog of a writer thinks he can drop off a play and just like that, I want to produce it? What an amateur to not seek my agent; I don't read scripts handed…ah, ha, ha. That's funny. Ho, ah, ha. That's not bad. Hmmmm. *Dogs,* huh? I think I can use this. I may have to never, ever contact Mister Paul Polk, eh? Could he be such an amateur, newbie writer that he didn't register it? Is he that much of a fool? Well. We're going to have to look into it as soon as we can."

A month later, newspapers announced a new play by Amandiss Hollington and it will open on Broadway. Amandiss 'pulled a few strings,' showed off his newest comedy to associate producers and they pushed their contacts to set-up a lavish and decadent opening for the musical, 'DOGS.' They spared no expense with promotions, sets, costumes, dog-costumes and casting. Actors like Bruce Dern and Strother Martin, not known for their singing abilities, have small parts in the production. Lead role went to Miss Carol Lynley, who proved to be an excellent singer in a few productions early in her career.

One evening, the doorbell rang at the Hollington

house and James opened the dark door. "Yes?"

Paul Polk said, "I have an appointment with Mr. Hollington. He is expecting me." Polk was a strong/young man who was very fit, athletic and handsome. Shorter hair than the style for the time. He had acted in a few bad movies and had modeled for years.

James was a little surprised, but was cordial. "Ah, then, please come this way. Who is it I should say is calling?"

"My name is…Smith. He knows who I am."

"Very good."

James brought the man through the house and onto a back porch where Amandiss sat on a recliner and was on the phone. James said, "Excuse me, sir. But you have an appointment with a Mister Smith?"

Hollington said into the large, black receiver: "Rudy. I'll call you back. Something's come up. Sorry." (click) He got to his feet, turned around and shouted: "No, I don't!" (to James) "You let this clown just walk in here!?"

"Relax…Hollington," Polk said, cool, casual, and cocky. "You know me. This will explain everything." He handed Amandiss a note.

The note read: *We need to talk alone or I will shoot you dead with the gun in my pocket.*

The producer and writer closed his eyes and changed his attitude. He calmly said: "I apologize, James. I do remember the appointment, now that I think about it. Me and, ah, *Mr. Smith* have some private matters to discuss. You can leave for the evening, James."

"Are you sure it's alright, sir?"

"Yes, yes. Run along, now." He smiled.

"Very good." The servant left the room.

A moment later, Amandiss sadly said, "I don't have much money in the house…"

"I don't want your money!" Peter snapped back, quickly.

"What do you want?"

"I want credit for the play you stole!"

"Ha, ha. Which one was that, my boy; I've stolen so many."

Paul Polk was angry and took out a gun from his vest. He pointed it directly at the older man and said: "Dogs."

"The new one! Yes, I remember now, now I know who I'm dealing with, eh? Ha, ha." Hollington laughed. He sat back down on the porch recliner and turned it and faced the young man. "Ha, ha! You're the one. The fool! Don't you know anything, young Mr. Polk? You have to register the scripts for plays. I've done nothing wrong! You see, sir, what I've done is done everyday to stupid, ignorants that don't protect their material. I registered it under my name, and that's all that really matters. Even if you can prove it was your original concept…ha, you gave it to me! You left it on my door and said: here! I was absolutely within my rights to copyright it as mine. You didn't do that. If you'd only done that first, I wouldn't have a leg to stand on. This is why *agents* must be involved. Again, you didn't do that. That's just…too bad, boy." He smiled as if in total control.

Paul kept the pistol trained on Hollington's head. "I'm not sure you know the situation you're in, Mr. Hollington!? I'm going to blow your head off if I don't get credit, or recognition, or a lot of money, or something, right now!!"

The man replied as if he didn't care to live. "With that small gun? Blow me away, then! I can size people up in a second. You're no killer. You're trying to scare me so I give you what you think you deserve. But I know my legal rights, Pete, I mean Paul, and I don't have to give you a damn thing! *Shoot!* I know you won't; you'll be a murderer. You'll get caught, your life will be ruined and you still won't be known for being the writer of Dogs. Ha!"

Paul dropped his arm and felt in his heart: *The bastard was right. I screwed up big time. But I can't let him get away with this. I can't let him get away Scott-free!* Polk aimed the gun at his leg and pulled the trigger! BANG!

"Damn you, bitch!!" Hollington screamed as blood poured out of his right leg. "Fuck!" He fell to the floor. "Oh, you mother-fucker, bitch, bastard!"

Paul panicked and ran out of the house.

Days later, the play at the Crowley Theatre opened and radio promos, TV ads, billboards, all announced 'DOGS' was coming and will be a "howling success!" It was the first time a Hollington-written play ever reached center stage Broadway and curious crowds wanted to see it. (Much of the crowd was high, especially celebrities who were given free tickets). Opening night went very well, at first. Strother Martin and Bruce Dern, as singing dogs, surprised a lot of people as they sang appealing tunes like: 'Give me the bone,' 'Poppa ooh mile, mile' and 'Flea Scratch, Flea Scratch.' When the Second Act was nearly finished, a horrible tragedy occurred onstage...

One of the extra "dogs" in the back of the set was in

the perfect spot during the 'Doghouse Blues' number – to be struck on the head from a ceiling sandbag that was not a sandbag. There were instant screams as a few of the *dogs* next to the female extra witnessed her face: *it busted apart and squirted blood!*

The curtain closed at a time it wasn't supposed to close, which blocked the view of the stage. Soon, one of the actors walked in front of the curtain and explained to the audience: "There has been a terrible accident. Please don't be alarmed, ladies and gentlemen. We are seeing to the matter. Apparently, one of the actors had a stroke or fainting spell. We have called an ambulance. The show will go on with Act 3 in approximately a half hour. We are very sorry for the interruption and hope you will understand the situation. Thank you."

An hour passed and the curtain went up. Hardly anyone left. They stayed and wanted to see the show. Whispers in the crowd: "I saw something fall from the roof. Then the screams." "Yeah, I saw it too. Like a part of the ceiling fell." 'If that's true, it was no heart attack." "We'll read about it tomorrow. Wonder how they'll explain it?"

Opening night was over. The story of *Dogs* was: Rich dogs with good homes in Dogtown were challenged to a fight by homeless, poor dogs from the street. Each sent a representative as a champion. If the rich dog won, all the gang-dogs would leave the area and never bother the dogs with homes ever again. And the winner got the beautiful Connie (Lynley) as their own mate. The story ends with Connie and Alpha-male dog, Butch (actor, Rex Reason) together and in love in a big mansion with no more problems from dogs on the street.

The reviews were good. Everything was wonderful in the show, until the extra dog's death. The tragic death made the news and the public was told: *A sandbag accidently fell from ceiling rafters and crushed the skull of one of the actors.* The public was not told that a heavy metal rod inside the sandbag was the real means of death. Sand would never have killed. People, via the news, were told it was an accident, but police officials and certain insiders knew it was murder.

Days before the death of the extra, Amandiss was alone onstage at the Crowley Theatre and checked the lighting. He turned a number of large spotlights to accentuate the centerstage. A young man suddenly walked out of the dark shadows. It was Paul Polk.

"My God, it's you!"

Paul said, "Amandiss! What kind of name is Amandiss, anyway?"

"It's a royal name. I'm from royal bloodlines. Now what the fuck are you doing here, boy?! I guess I should carry a gun as well, huh? Decided to kill me, did you? Ha! That'll be the day. Oh, thanks for the limp, fucker." Hollington was sure of himself. "You can't threaten me or intimidate me...now, what?!!"

Polk answered, "I'm here to tell you I will never let go of this! I am ruined, financially. All this hoopla, the ads, the billboards on buses! *Because of me!* I should be sharing in it and sharing in the big profits!" Paul was distraught, nervous and shook somewhat. He wiped sweat from his face.

Amandiss said, "You better kill me now, boy. Now I know to have bodyguards with me at all times. I have a private eye that will find you, my friend; you'll be arrested for stalking, Paul Polk!" Hollington put up a confident front, but inside he was scared.

"Yeah, I'm leaving now. I only wanted to tell you, as long as you operate from this theater, I will be like a phantom in the wind, watching you; you will feel me in the air, behind the curtains. Maybe I'll gaslight you into a confession, eh? Drive you so crazy, you'll crack? I will never let it go until you confess and give me satisfaction. I know where you live and can get inside your place as easy as I got inside the theater, Mister Hollington. Just speak…*and I will hear you.*"

Hollington got even more scared when he heard the young man's creepy voice and looked deep into his glassy eyes. The boy was nuts! Maybe it was paranoia; maybe it was all of the cocaine? Something got a hold of Amandiss Hollington and controlled his actions. He saw what was behind the boy: a tub of dry ice used for special-effects. Suddenly, he pushed the boy who tripped and fell into a tub!

"Aaaaugh! Ahh! Aaaaaaa!!!" Paul Polk was in extreme pain. ***His head and the top portion of his body smashed against the dry ice and the pain was more than he could take!*** He screamed, grabbed his head and ran through a backstage corridor and into darkness and madness~.

Dogs was in its second week and was a smash hit! The death on opening night was smoothed over as an "accident" and forgotten. Hollington now carried a pistol, a 45 caliber. He thought that was as good as a bodyguard. *I could always shoot him when he appears again, my stalker. Yes, it could all come out; how he gave me his play to produce. I liked it, made phone calls and it turned out fabulous, the first week, anyway. But Polk tried to extort money out of me that he was not entitled to. Then when he threatened me with his gun; that was too much. He was a lunatic psycho, for sure! We fought for the gun and it went off! I had to defend myself and also will remember to put his prints on my gun. I have his note. I have James who will testify that he barged into my home. I had to shoot him! He was insane!*

Backstage, Hollington met with his agent: Murph. Murph told Amandiss, "I was sure Dogs was dead the first night. *Jesus Christ,* an iron bar in a sandbag? The killer had to be right on top of that person. He aimed, dropped the bag and squa-doosh..."

"Or she?"

"What?" Murph asked.

"Maybe the killer's a woman?"

"Oh, yeah. But what babe would be in your rafters knocking off the actors, eh? What I'm tellin' youse is...we're doing a super box office. You saw how massive the crowds are? They think there might be another 'accident,' like it's a jinxed production...?"

"I heard that on the news, Murph. Whoever is spreading the rumor that another death might occur and all kinds of things have gone wrong, I want to thank that guy..."

"Or gal, ha, ha..."

"Or gal." Hollington continued: "...Cause it's been *great for business!* It's been mentioned in the reviews of Dogs: even the possibility of a murder cover-up has been fantastic for us and the backers. Ha, ha. Maybe we need another murder, eh? To really pack them in? New York. Only in New York. They like to see building jumpers jump, you know what I mean, Murph?"

"Ha, ha. I do. Ah...."

The playwright and agent heard a bit of Rex Reason (the Butch-character in the show) in costume who sang a bit of Dog House Blues:

"I'm the top dog, like the top cat, but I know exactly where it's at! We get high on the East Side, we get high on the West Side, but it's never quite like that! Subways are listening, and skyscrapers are glistening! Everyone is waiting for war, war, war! What does it really matter? When you hear the chatter and the only motive is to score more, more, more!"

Peacenik, Connie (Lynley) entered in her white fur suit and sang:

"I....don't know how to love you. When you speak of war, what is it for? Barking is over. Biting is coming, teeth and claws are grinding, and I'm going out, out, out of my freaking mind! If I were ever to lose you. Lose you..."

Carol Lindley was the last one out of the theater one evening after a rehearsal, still in her dressing room. She thought she was alone until she heard a piano that played on the mainstage. She walked there and saw a man in a white mask. How mysterious: one spotlight in the darkness. He played a song she'd never heard and it was beautiful. *What an enchanting melody,* she thought. She walked closer and closer to him. He did not see or hear here; he was completely in a state of rapture as he played the original song. He wore a black cape and was immaculately dressed in a tuxedo.

From behind him, she was so close she could touch the masked pianist. Then a devilish thought struck the actress. She felt playful near the sounds of such sweet music…*Should I? It might be a cute way to say 'hi' and to say that I love what you're playing?*

Carol reached from behind and pulled his mask off!

He turned and his face was *monstrous!* Scarred by extreme cold, lines etched his withered face. He lost most of his hair. The once handsome man was now a hideous monster! His eyes bugged out in rage! His black arm reached out from under the cape.

She screamed, fell to the floor and passed out…

Later, she regained semi-consciousness, but it was a slow process. Her lovely arms and legs moved, slightly. Her eyes were closed. She was still in a hazy dream-state. He brushed her blonde hair with his hand. She felt something soft on her cheek. Carol smiled. She touched the hand that gently stroked her cheek and held it for a while. Slowly, she opened her eyes and saw him over her. She wasn't frightened; she was cautious. He wore a white mask. Behind the mask, he smiled. She liked his blue eyes. It was as if she looked into his soul. Was the pianist a good man? She wasn't sure.

"You play divinely, sir. What was the name of the song?"

"Lime."

"Ha, uh." Then Carol was near tears. "I…I am very, very sorry. I mean about…what happened to you. What's your name?"

His voice was a comforting voice. He replied, "Paul."

"Paul." She smiled. "Did you write the song you were playing?"

"I did," he answered.

"Beautiful," was her comment.

He returned the compliment, "I've seen you act in movies before, but I've never heard you sing. You can really sing. You have a wonderful voice, Miss Lindley…"

"Carol."

"Carol."

Dogs was in its second month and the Crowley Theatre was nearly filled to capacity show after show, but not as much as it was in its first month. Sales had plateaued and were a bit down. Murph was worried that this was a bad sign of things to come and *Dogs* might close much sooner than expected.

Almost on cue, a shocking incident happened right in front of a 3-quarter crowd, one particular Saturday night in New York City. In the middle of Act 3, just before the finale of the War, during a quiet moment, a side curtain on the left of the stage ripped down from the top. And ripped, and ripped, and ripped farther down until it split the curtain in two halves. After a hush that got everyone's attention, *a man in a catsuit* swung out of the opening from a rope. Tied from the high rafters, the rope swung back and forth over the front of the stage. At first, people thought it was part of the theater play; a surprise attack, possibly? But no. Screams and more screams echoed in the theater when more and more people realized the thing that swung out was not a mannequin; *it was a real body that dripped blood!*

One more time Carol Lindley was the last one in the theater, she thought. She stayed late on purpose. The actress pretended she had terrible trouble in the removal of her dog-costume. This was in the hopes: Paul might spring out from the darkness and speak with her once more. She was intrigued by him. Was it Beauty and the Beast? She felt terribly sorry for him. Did he have anything to do with one of the stagehands murdered, placed in a cat-suit and swung out over the stage? She had to know the truth.

Paul appeared in a mask and in the light from the back of her dressing room. He said, "Isn't it a sick joke that they put Willy in a catsuit? Like dogs did it, 'cos, you know? Dogs hate cats, right? What kind of sick, fucking mind would do such a thing? Actually, there are two choices who's the psycho-killer, Miss Lindley. Maybe it's my alter ego? Or, maybe it's *him?!"*

Carol did not hesitate. She asked seriously, "Did you have anything to do with the murder of Willy Drexler?"

Paul Polk's answer was a question: "Do you really believe my hands that played such sweet music could strangle and stab that poor boy?"

She asked, "How did you know he was strangled and stabbed?"

"Well, besides it only makes sense it happened that way...*I saw it!* I saw who killed your friend, Willy."

"Who did it?!" Miss Lindley asked with big, blue eyes.

"He pulled a cord that ripped the curtain, then tripped a sandbag that sent the rope out like a pendulum..."

"Who?!"

"Come now, Carol. Who else?" The man in black and in a black cape grabbed his mask and took it off as he bowed to her.

She bit her hand and avoided a scream. He was very scarred.

Paul then disappeared into the darkness, really

temporary walls that could be removed, which led to a thin crawlspace. In this way, the "phantom" maneuvered through the whole of Crowley Theatre. His strength and acrobats served him well as he often perched from the rafters. In black, no one saw his presence over the main stage and other rooms. But he saw. He was like Spiderman. He witnessed the dropped sandbag with an iron bar in it the first night – he also saw from a distance (night-scope) who killed the cat.

On the way home, in her car, Carol contemplated a few things about her mysterious Paul: *Was he crazy? Was he lying? After the suffering that man had to endure, it would drive anyone over the edge, yes? Who could live with so much disfiguration? An outcast from society. If he had something against the production or Mr. Hollington or anyone here, then maybe he is the madman doing this? Or, to really be far-out, what if Paul is an agent of chaos, like the CIA? He might not even have control of his mind and what he's doing...like a robot. Is he sabotaging the show to make it more profitable and have a long run? Are the agents doing this? Which ones? I don't know.*

Amandiss had his own private quarters in the theater, a room that Paul Polk bugged and also set up a video camera. He thought a video with sound could be the perfect instrument of revenge on Mr. Hollington. But what he found on the video shocked him to the core and he had to share it with Carol.

This time, Paul found out where she lived, *broke into her apartment and scared the shit out of the actress while she was in bed!*

"What are you doing here?!" she shouted.

"Please, forgive me, Carol. But you have to see this." He tossed the video recording on her bed. Paul knew she'd find the means to play it. He blew her a kiss and then left by way of the window.

"Bye," she said, dazed and confused.

The next day, she found the right machine and played the film.

The shocker was: Amandiss was locked in his theater room and was sure he was alone. Paul's camera recorded his actions in the mirror. He removed his usual, thick sweater. He undid the strap that held his breasts tight against his body. *Hollington had female breasts.* They were small breasts, but they were definitely female breasts. Carol and her agent, who provided the video machine, had a good laugh…until they realized who the real psycho-killer was. Hollington committed the murders so there was a controversy around *Dogs* and both tragedies surely boosted ticket sales. He had his first hit on Broadway and, at the same time, implicated a real Phantom of the Broadway show. Hollington (Duke of Ardale) was royalty, a secret tranny, which was why he lived such a solitary life, an unmarried loner. Was "A Man" diss and his financial connections behind all the publicity that surrounded *Dogs?* Even to the point that the public knew there was a killer in the Crowley Theatre! The Press said the theater had a killer, a "phantom." In the second month, after the second killing, the seats were once again filled. Would the Theater-Killer kill again during another performance? The public came to see.

Bruce Dern and Strother Martin wanted out and got

out of the play after the *cat was killed.* They were replaced. Rex Reason also wanted out, but stayed for Carol's sake. No one's heart was in their performances and the end of the show was certainly near.

It was felt among the cast and possibly felt among the audience, that this was the last performance of the blockbuster show, *Dogs.*

Rex and Carol performed the tasteful "dog" love-scene after the war. There were only minutes before the curtain fell. The music swelled to a high crescendo in the theater. Paul Polk covered his face, entered one of the balconies along with people who paid for their seats. Everyone was in a good mood, on their feet and cheered as the climax of the show was reached. And didn't notice him. But suddenly:

A loud gunshot was heard by the crowd! Then screams! People panicked and ran for the exits! *A body fell off the balcony* and into the audience below. It was Paul Polk. He was recognized by Hollington in his own private balcony directly across, and shot. It was a cocaine-driven act or maybe Amandiss simply realized it was his Last Act? He ran out the back way in paranoiac fear and was later caught by police.

Carol Lindley, with Rex Reason right behind her, dashed over to where Paul landed among the seats. He bled heavily in the chest, but was still alive and smiled. Paul said one word before he died: "Wuff."

Carol cried. She spoke to him as if he was not dead: "Paul! Paul, the video told me many things: Who the killer was and who really wrote *Dogs!* People will find out the truth; he did this to you. Ugh. You wrote the play and Hollington stole it. Wuff to you too, Paul."

2
Sky Captain and the World Beyond

"That's hard to believe, Dex! You're telling me the Rocketeers and the Bulleteers have joined forces?! That's horrible news! I thought they were mortal enemies?" Joe Sullivan, otherwise known as 'Sky Captain,' shouted over his radio. He was grounded, inside an opium den [wild goose chase] with his trusty plane parked outside.

At the base was Dex, a young/scientific genius and

Joe's close friend. He replied on the radio: *"Captain, it blew me away too! Far as I can tell, they want to bait you; draw you into an area, cut you off, then bullet the piss out of you, man!"*

Sky Captain said, "That's, ah, let's see, about 40 missile-planes, when you combine both air-forces, eh? I don't like the odds, Dex! Especially when you figure they fly *faster* than me in my Tiger. Tell me, you think they've buried the hatchet and put away their famous feud because of me?"

"Looks that way, Cap. Don't do it, sir! Don't go to them. You barely survived when the Rocketeers' missile-planes hit Tiger last time. That was 20 planes! Now, double that, Cap! Wait for help! Without any other support, you're a dead duck…"

"Right about that, Dex. They don't care about the missiles they drive or their own lives! They're set on kamikaze-ing me, just to knock me out of the sky and claim me as a trophy, aye?" Joe ran out of the Chinese temple and headed for his plane.

"You got it. Now come back to base; don't go to them…"

"Dex, you know I'm going to go to them," Joe said in a low voice.

"Oh, shit. No, Cap. Why don't you ever listen to me?!"

"I always listen to you! But, but, right now…I'm feeling very Polly Perkins and…uh, *gonna go headlong into it!* You know, I miss the girl…"

"WHY?!" Dex screamed over the mic…

"Why do I miss 'er? I dunno, Dex. That stupid smile of hers. I never know what she's gonna say, her dumb questions and that irritating, irritating voice…"

"NO!! No, no! Why face the Bulleteers and Rocketeers alone?!"

"Oh…ah, let's see? …Because it's a challenge, eh? Wish me luck, Dex! Sky Captain, over and out…" (click).

"God, no. No, no. Foolish man. I don't think he knows how damn serious this is. One day, he's not going to fly home. I have a very bad feeling about this."

A short time later, before any help came from base, Sky Captain and Tiger reached a 'hornet's nest' of about 40 enemy missile-planes. The ships turned toward the Captain and aimed trajectories to crash into his craft.

Special, wide-caliber, Jet Bullets (Dex developed) that the Tiger shot were extremely potent. They could riddle an airplane and knock it out of the sky in seconds. Joe shot down the closest missile-plane to him in a half minute! But there were far too many of the enemy in the sky a little farther away. Captain's Tiger wasn't going to make it being this outnumbered.

"What the hell? You only have 9 lives," Joe said as he adjusted his goggles, grit his teeth and <u>fired and fired and fired Jet Bullets</u>! Then…

<u>Time stopped</u>.

Everything stopped! Reality: planes in the sky, zeppelins on the horizon, troops on the ground and big, white, billowy clouds above… Froze! Nothing moved at all. Except people.

Joe laughed. "Ha, ha. This is grand! HA!! The missile-men are stranded in the air, stationary, just like me? Ha! Gee, look at that. More had turned to me I didn't see. Oh, I woulda been bulleted to hell if not for, if not for. I guess, this is a lucky break for me that the pause freeze-frame happened." Joe looked up. "I thank the lucky stars!"

Sky Captain removed his goggles and pilot's cap. He opened the cockpit and made Tiger a convertible. Joe stood up tall, breathed gulps of air, in and out, which seemed to move. He walked out on the wing and sat down. There was a quiet stillness now, but less than a minute ago when he heard his loud engine and the engines of missile-planes. Sun shined. It was a lovely, peaceful, frozen dogfight. Nice.

Out of all the stationary things, something moved in the air, a few miles away. The object got closer. Its engine was clearly heard: another plane, one that functioned and flew through the air. Not a missile-plane. It was…it was…

"Oh, no," Sky Captain exhaled and nearly gagged. It was: "Polly Purebread! I mean, Polly Perkins, and you're flying one of our X4Ks and, ha, ha! Who do I see riding in back? Franky!?"

The slick, shiny, dark-green, X4k smoothly came closer and closer and parked in the air right alongside the Tiger. Polly popped the cockpit glass as well.

Joe waved to the girls then asked Franky, "You let her drive? You really think that was wise, Francesca?"

"Ha, ha," from Polly, sarcastically.

Franky shrugged. "Hello, Joseph! Tell me. Why are you and the bullet brothers over there hovering in midair, stuck, and we girls, apparently, are not?"

"I thought you could tell me?! No? Any ideas, Miss Perkins?"

"I have no clue. Although, it is a big story. See, brought my camera." Polly held it up and waved it a bit.

Joe said, "It's times like these…I wish I had Dex

here. Someone with a few answers." He thought to call base on the radio, when…

DEX APPEARED! In the seat behind Joe. Dex materialized into solid matter. His eyes widened and he exclaimed: "Whoa!"

Joe acted cool and stated, "I was just about to call you, Dex. Ha."

Dex was dazed. "Wh-why am I…who, who put me here?"

Suddenly, *bullets were fired* from the bullet-men and the rocket-men! They popped their glass-bubbles as well and fired shots from handheld pistols!

"Hey! Hey!"

"Duck!

"They're firing!"

Joe was cool and told Polly, "Just close the glass bubble! It's bulletproof." She did and he did.

Joe turned on the radio so the girls could hear the conversation. But there wasn't much of a talk because Dex, Joe, Franky and Polly *disappeared!* They were beamed aboard a spacecraft that was in high Earth orbit. A ship from the future.

When the foursome became physical, conscious and lucid…

They understood they were in a spaceship because it definitely appeared like one, especially since stars and black space were seen out of round portals. The section they were in looked like a large, round hangar. A few odd, small ships were next to closed, exterior portals. The hangar was sparse, dark and unappealing. Then they heard footsteps. Two people approach them:

One looked exactly like Joe! He could have been his twin brother, only he wore cool/colorful, futuristic clothes. Light, shiny, spandex? The other person wasn't quite human. He had large, humanish eyes. He was no more than 5-foot high and green. He had gills on the side of his head. Outside of that, the little humanoid was perfectly normal.

"Go say hi to yourself, Captain," Dex urged Joe.

Joe from 1954 walked to modern Joe and they both clasped hands vigorously and smiled. Modern Joe told Joe and the gang: "In some cases when parallels meet, they *explode* in an antimatter explosion. But we didn't do that, ha."

Dex and Joe glanced at each other. Dex said, "That's good."

"Bet you fellas, and ladies, would like to know what's going on?" the charming/smiling, modern Joe stated.

"Bet you fellas were behind the strange hijinks back there?" Sky Captain said.

"Ha, you guessed it, Joe." Joe said.

Polly moved closer, real close to the green 'alien,' and…

[snap] She had 5 shots left in her camera.

"Damn" the creature said and covered his eyes. He had a funny voice.

"You shouldn't have done that, Polly. Those future eyes we'll all receive eventually, are really sensitive."

"I'll be fine" he said. "I should have anticipated her move."

Joe looked at his double. He wanted clarity. "You're me?"

"I'm you in the future. Seven hundred and twenty-one years in the future, to be exact."

"Blimey!" Commander Cook (Franky) expressed. She got to the point and said: "Why are we 'ere, future Joseph, and 'is little friend?"

Modern Joe replied in a serious tone: "We need you."

The creature that appeared as an alien, that was not an alien, said: *"We need you, desperately."*

"To do wot?" Franky asked.

"Well, we're going to have to show you." Cool Joe, in shiny clothes, said. "Please. Come this way."

"Whoa. Look at that, Joe." Dex marveled at the small spaceships parked near curved walls. "Imagine flying one of them, Cap! We'd have to call you Space Captain, eh?"

Modern Joe laughed and said, "Ha, ha. That's what they call me! I'm otherwise known as 'Space Captain.' And I love it…"

"Oh, boy."

Polly said, "I don't know if I could take two of them…"

"I think I could handle two of them, aye?" Franky said, made a sexy face and blew them a kiss.

Everyone smiled at the sexual innuendo. Not Polly; she smirked and made a weird face.

"Franky! I just noticed what's odd about you," Joe from the past said.

"Wot?"

"Ha, ha. Your eyepatch is on *the wrong eye!* It was on the right eye, and now, it's on the left eye? Explain, please…" Sullivan was puzzled.

She replied, "All these fantastic things around us and you want to know about my eye?"

"Yeah, yeah," he said and shook his head. "What happened?"

"My right eye got better and my left eye got injured. Does that explain it?"

"Good to know. Good to know." He smiled.

Dex wanted answers and asked, "Before you show us, can you tell us more of what we're doing here, while we're walking?"

Future Joe answered, "Sure. Have you ever seen the old serial, Buck Rogers, or, or, Flash Gordon? Or movies of them?"

"Ah, no, never heard of them."

Dex asked, "Should we know them?"

The green creature turned to Space Captain and said, *"They're from a different universe. In a sense, they're the Rogers and Gordon of this world..."*

"Ah. Okay, well in those 'movies,' they jumped into the future, and lo and behold, they saved the World Beyond their time! It didn't make sense for, you could say, *primitives* from the past to solve the problem in the world of the future, but they did..."

The green humanoid continued the talk, *"Today, in our time, we also face a grave problem, more than that, a **possible extinction!** Our Prime Source has shown us this truth...that you, and only you people, will be our saviors in the end."*

"Us?" Polly questioned.

Dex was upset and asked, "Wait a minute. What's fictional movies, like you said Buck Rodgers and Flash were, have anything to do with us, or *reality?!"*

"Ha, ha, ha!" Space Captain laughed and said, "It's, ah, very complicated. But after we show you a few items, I think you'll understand."

"Well, answer me this – who's the green guy?" Dex asked.

"Ha, ha!" Future Joe laughed.

The green humanoid said, *"I thought you were smarter than that, Dex. I'm you, of course. Space Captain's trusty and loyal sidekick…"*

"Shazam!!" Dex said in utter amazement. "I did always want to be green."

The green Dex said, *"Call me Dexter, to avoid confusion…"*

"Who's confused?" Polly said.

In the ship's laboratory, and later in time, a few truths were explained to the foursome from the past. But the biggest shock and purpose for the kidnapping was still to come…

"This is Doctor Elias Heur," Space Captain said to the gang.

"Hello."

"It's a pleasure."

"Doctor.

"Dexter added: *"Dr. Huer here and myself might be the smartest humans on the planet, and that is with respect to our Prime Source. And we can't stop the doomsday that's ahead…"*

"Doomsday?" Sky Captain repeated. Still hadn't sunk in.

Dex said, "Dexter said a grave problem and *possible extinction.* Can you explain, please?"

"I thought it had been explained to you?" The doctor looked at Joe and Dexter from his own time.

They shook their heads for no.

Dexter said: *"We thought it best if you explained to them, sir."*

"I see. Then I will. All of you, gather around this

machine over here and look at the front of the scope." The doctor directed them to another part of the lab a short distance away. "Galileo would be proud of this. No peephole, eh? It is a real tele-scope." The device projected a 3D space of exactly what it was focused on millions of miles out into space. The 3D volume of space can be moved back and forth, side to side and easily focused in on any star system.

"Fascinating," Dex said. Joe and the girls agreed.

"Right. We've come a long way since your time with these types of telescopes..."

"Doomsday! Doctor?" Franky reminded the old man with a lot of white hair.

"Right, right. We have no time to lose. No one can explain why this is happening, but it's happening."

"Wot?"

Dr. Huer turned a small dial which shot the device's focus billions of lightyears in distance! The easy-view tele-scope displayed a neighboring galaxy's star pattern on one side of the 3D screen and on the other side...was *nothing,* a **blackness**, and was discovered to be a total emptiness.

There were movements. Dr. Huer made the view even closer. It was as if the blackness, the Nothing, *ate star systems and turned them to nothing at an incredibly fast rate!!*

Dex asked Dexter, very seriously, "How much time do we have?"

Dexter answered, "Less than a week, Prime Source has estimated. Nothing approaches faster and faster. PS has also informed our fearful world that we are doomed unless me, you, all of us, come up with something fast, before total extinction...so we have to get cracking..."

Joe from 1954 was stunned and expressed, "Hold on. There are infinite galaxies; it goes on forever. There are galactic clusters, clusters of clusters, and…"

Dexter said sadly, "No more, my friends. Nothing exists of the World Beyond our galactic neighborhood. Yesterday, there were 25 galaxies in existence, the closest ones to us. Today, there are only the LMC System, Antlia 2, Andromeda, the Magellanic Clouds, and who knows tomorrow? Nothing might be devouring the Milky Way, tomorrow?"

"That's horrendous," Polly said in fear and shook a little. "How, how do y-you suppose we…get cracking?"

Joe from 2675 stated a fine idea: "I say, we split up. It's Dex and Dexter that'll sort everything out, I'm sure." (smiled) "Let's leave me, Dr. Huer and the Prime Source out of it! I think that's the ticket because our answers have been nil, so far. We need a *different angle* to solve the problem of the cosmos disappearing. That's the key and I think your Dex, along with our Dexter, will find the answer we need. Dexter has saved the world before; I'm sure he'll do it again." Space Captain pointed at Dex. "You're the answer, Dex. You're the X-factor and missing element in the formula, yes? I have confidence now. We get cracking by leaving them alone, put them in an isolated Think Tank, a Big/Black Box, aye?"

"What do *we* do?" Joe asked the more aware version of himself.

"We wait."

"Wait?" Polly asked, with spunk. "I don't like waiting. Not in my nature." She took a photo of Doctor Heur with his tele-scope and a few other wild machines in the background. She only had 2 left.

Dr. Huer turned to Dexter and asked him, "Do we

need to tell them about the war between the Artificial Intelligence and the Natural Intelligence, or should we leave that for another time?"

Green Dexter with gills on the side of his head, replied, "We'll leave that for another time."

Next day came and the breaking news was awful: *The Nothing started obliterating the Milky Way! There were no other galaxies in the universe and the last galaxy shrank hour to hour!*

Dex and Dexter were in their Think Tank and they tossed around theories, formulae, ideas and curious thoughts: *What would Nikola Tesla do at a time like this? What about Theodor Adorno? Al Beliek, or the Grompa from Barnard's Star?*

"Do you have anything yet, boys?!" and other comments were shouted at the tank by the Joes and the girls.

"Nothing yet!" Dexter shouted from inside. "But Dex thinks he has something…"

"Good boy, Dex," Sky Captain said with a confident smile. "They're gonna save the Earth; he always does! I have no doubt."

Commander Cook with the eyepatch, kissed Joe from 2675 and explained: "It was for good luck."

The group outside of the Think Tank all smiled. Even Huer.

Both Joes got frustrated at the same time and yelled in the direction of the big, black box: "What have you got?!!"

The Dexs emerged and went directly into an explanation of a possible solution:

"Okay!" Dex said, excitedly. "Dexter first showed

me on his wrist screen what a Norcavata Machine is…"

"What's a Norcavata Machine?" Joe from the '50s asked.

Dexter responded: "We pulled a fictional device from a television show you know nothing of; made it into a physical reality. Prime Source explained: Because of the nature of the TV device, what it supposedly was – that made it possible to crossover into our reality. It sends people to various realities. I quickly worked on it…"

Dex jumped in with high energy, "Yeah! I'm great, I mean, he's great! He showed me a minute of the show; it's called Star Trek, and a Mr. Atos had an Atavacron Machine. I knew as soon as I saw it – if he could cross it over onto this side and make it a physical reality and I could get my grubbies on it, with their tools…hell, I could make it work IN REVERSE…"

"Huh?"

"What?"

"I don't follow."

Dexter was going to explain, then he waved and gave the privilege to Dex.

Dex said, "It's done! I turned it into, with their help, I turned it into a Norcavata Machine!"

"We'd have never thought of it," Dexter confessed and rubbed his gills.

"A what?" Joe from 2675 didn't know. "And I'm Space Captain."

Dex said, "The reverse of what was seen in the show. Now. Instead of pulling things from movies and TV shows into our reality…it's the reverse. *We* can go into the movies, films, TV shows, HA, HA!!!" Dex was overly psyched, really overjoyed, as if this was the ultimate answer to the coming Doomsday…

But the gang just didn't see it. They did not understand: How a real Norcavata Machine answers their prayers and the prayers of other lifeforms in the Milky Way.

"Huh?"

"What?"

"Run that by me again."

Doctor Huer figured it out and he was amazed. He expressed, "You don't mean? You don't really mean we can go into films and television programs, be an actual part of the fiction and fantasy?"

"Precisely," Dexter said proudly, with hands on his small hips. The War between the Intelligences is over. There's no solution, only escape. The machines cannot escape, I don't think. But we all can! Norcavatas are being duplicated and sent out, with instructions."

"Hold on a moment, gentlemen," Franky said. "So, you don't have a plan to save the world, to maybe go back in time and bring back the World Beyond the galaxy? It's only a plan to save our asses by becoming characters in old stories?"

Dex told Francesca, sincerely, "That's the best we got Franky, and frankly, there really wasn't another alternative to oblivion. Many star systems might find their own solution in time. This is ours. As they say in movies, 'it's our only hope.'"

Polly Perkins snapped a picture of her Joe. The look on his face was priceless. He'd wind up as a character in a movie or on a TV show. She wondered what he'd choose. *What would I choose?* She had one shot left and would save that for the world of tomorrow.

They had one more day until Earth's doomsday. In that time, the gang from the past and all citizens from

2675...*reviewed movies on their screens and picked which fictional characters and situations they could "step into" and motivate.* Earthlings will be saved. And it was thanks to Dex Dearborn. Here were the gang's fictional choices and the roles (for the rest of their lives) they chose:

Joe transitioned to Sam from 'Cheers.'

Polly transitioned to Diane from 'Cheers.'

Future Joe transitioned into Superman.

Franky transitioned into Sigourney Weaver who settled down after her first experience with xenomorph aliens, did not return to space, but instead: Assumed the identity of Lois Lane, who worked as a reporter on the Daily Planet, along with Clark Kent.

Dexter transitioned into Buck Rogers. He enjoyed his new identity very much and could not wait for fantastic adventures to come. Although, he missed breathing underwater, his skin color and his terrific, enhanced eyesight.

Dex transitioned into Flash Gordon! Maybe he was tired of being the second banana, always in the shadow of Joe? A little like Robin, always second chair to Batman (he learned when he searched for an eternal place to exist in comic books). Dex thought of a question; he did not know the answer: *When you are the character in a film or TV production, you're real, aren't you? Are you only a cartoon? Or are you living, breathing flesh and blood?* The Boy Wonder was not sure. "Could I die? Die by Ming's electro-blasts from one of his stupid spaceships held up by strings? Or at the hands of a Hawkman? Did I make the right choice? I could have been Star-Lord, or *Shazam!*"

3
Panday

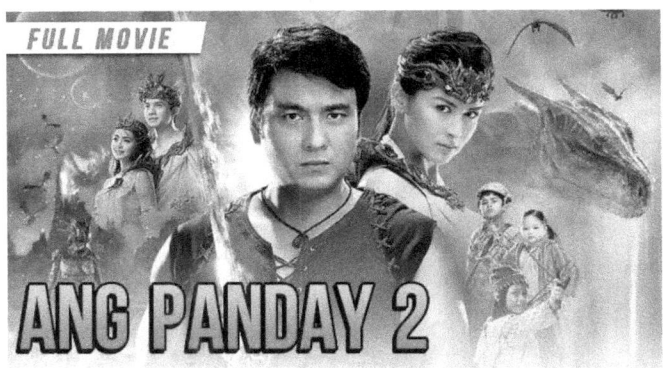

A film was released in Japan and China called **"PANDAY"** in 2015. The film was nothing extraordinary or any different from your average Shogun, Samurai, or Kaiju-types of movies. It was odd that a film (let alone a planned series of big-budget films) was co-funded, co-produced by China and Japan. Critics and audiences believed it was a clever "marketing scheme" as well as the use of real Pandas in its promotion. It was highly-pushed, but not well-received. True critics, not paid critics, blasted the acting, the writing, the special-effects of giant monsters, the direction, the editing, the sound and music were all harshly criticized.

The Panday story involved a revolutionary named Ang, who was fed up with an insane new mandate that the 7-day week will now consist of an 8th day called: "Panday." On that day, 4 times a month, from now on: **You are legally allowed to kill as many people as you want!** Panday served multiple purposes for the State: 1) The main purpose was population-control. There were far too many citizens and lowlife, homeless beggars in the streets. A means to clean-up the cities and villages. 2) To alleviate the build-up of tension and stress from long hours worked in the fields. 3) To have *fun,* to get your "kicks" in a new wave of an exciting, thrilling and deadly Sport.

The Ang-character led a small group of men that took on the feared Emperor and the powerful empire. His movement gained more and more support. Soon, hundreds of rebels became thousands of rebels that fought to free all people against the tyranny of power-mad fascists. Ang's revolution overthrew the Old Order and established a fair and free world for all Children of Tomorrow.

The first Panday film was followed by a sequel with a better script, larger budget, better special-effects, big-name actors and very impressive reviews. The theme was the same: an individual on the side of truth can turn corruption into freedom. In a few years, Panday was a Chinese and Japanese institution with a Part 3 and Part 4, etc.

Panday was also a massive success in London, Rome, New York, heavily-pushed and very popular among the youth. There were a series of Panday films especially designed for *young children and girls*. Critics were quick and said: "Yes, the revolution's cause is just, but viewers see endless SLAUGHTER! Boys, girls, all citizens everywhere, took up swords and other arms and killed the 'bad guys' in the name of goodness and righteousness…but, the masses were still KILLING, the very principle they sought to prevent. The films were all-WAR. Where was peace and love and understanding? Only for a moment at the very end of the films?" Most true critics thrashed each installment of the franchise: "The giant monsters are gone; great special-effects are gone. Now filmmakers have children killing children, instructing them on how to kill. It's all violence now, violence for a good cause, of course. That's what Panday has become as it reaches a global audience. It's wrong for young crowds."

In Los Angeles, within Hollywood High School, a speaker spoke to the junior and senior classes in the large auditorium. Onstage was Rosalie Williams, a representative of the Parents and Teachers Association. The talk was about the psychological effects of the popular Panday series that has spread west from the east…

"Young people, it is so easy to be caught up in mob-mentality. What I mean by that is simply doing what everyone else is doing. You see everyone doing it, whatever that be, and you think it's Okay to do it too. What if what you're doing is wrong? Ever stop to consider that? What if the discrimination or hatred you're dispensing, that everyone is doing, is not only wrong, but *terrible?!* You young boys and girls cannot wait to get your tattoos! Why? Because all of you have these marks now and to fit in, you feel you must have them too? Instead of standing up as an individual and being different, you're all the same. You all have phones now and it would be unthinkable for you not to have them. Remember the days when people read books, yes, for entertainment and information, and not used the computer? Now, teachers don't say: 'Open your books, class.' Books are being phased out, cancelled! So is individualism, uniqueness and uniqueness…oh, there's a hand up. Yes?"

"Miss…Williams?"

"It's Mrs."

"Mrs. Williams. The billboard says this was about Panday. I don't see the connection. When are you going to mention the Panday movies?" Other students in the auditorium agreed.

She replied, "I want to make a point first…"

"Okay." Everyone listened closely.

Mrs. Williams asked, "I want to take a survey. You either like the Deadpool movies or you don't like the Deadpool movies. If you're indifferent, don't care or have no opinion, don't raise your hand. Raise your hand if you like Deadpool movies, think they're funny and enjoy seeing them?"

Most of the juniors and seniors of Hollywood High raised their hands.

"How many of you absolutely do not like Deadpool movies and wouldn't be caught dead seeing one?"

Only a handful of students raised their hands.

Rosalie Williams immediately applauded the few boys and girls. "I thought so. I appreciate you brave students that go against the tide, the *tsunami;* it's a metaphor for what most of you think. No matter what morality or common sense is before you, you will chuck it all away for popularity, conformity and to be like everyone else." The PTA rep stared back at the boy who expressed the question: "Maybe I haven't made my point to you? How my words relate to Panday is…I've taken other surveys. I want to understand what you see in Panday, what is it that excites your juices about it? Why do you all, mostly, love it? Is it the excitement? The fast and furious action? Marching to the drums of freedom, like many did in the '60s? Or. Or, is it the gore, the blood, the killing? The war? Is violence why you watch Panday and its other incarnations over and over again? In surveys, I've found out that's why you watch it: *the blood and gore,* not the 'principles of freedom' that filmmakers and some critics believe have value in it. You don't think the repetition of violent images for children, and acted out by children, has a direct negative/nasty effect on society? We're here to discuss. Speak up, if you have anything to say."

One senior, with glasses and head of the Student Council, said, "That's an old argument, Mrs. Williams. Frank Zappa arguing censorship before Congress. The arguments against pornography: does what we see in movies or hear in songs cause bad behaviors in society?"

"Exactly. There's plenty of mothers and fathers that believe they do," she replied.

"And the counterpoint is: they don't and you're making too much of it…"

"Yeah."

"Yeah." The crowd agreed with the student.

Another spoke up and said, "We're being treated like children. We're not so incredibly dumb to go out and do what we see on TV or in movies."

"Some of us…"

A few laughs.

"I'm very glad to hear that, students," Mrs. Williams said. "We're not trying to censor you. It's guidance. I know you don't want to hear that you'll feel differently when you are adults, when you have children of your own…but you will. You'll feel that your mothers and fathers weren't so bad. You'll become your own versions of your parents…"

[Stirrings and murmurs in the audience].

"I know that's not the greatest news you want to hear. But you will have children and you want to care for them and sincerely protect them from harm. Physical harm, mental harm. You won't want them abused. You'll watch what they watch and listen to what they listen to. Panday is harmful and damaging. It did not start that way; the second movie hooked a lot of kids. The youth of the west were curious and wanted to see what all the excitement was about. It's understandable. But to go get weapons, sword fight in real life? Is that what's next? Panday underground Fight Clubs…?"

"Yeah!"

A few students cheered.

"Yeah, fight clubs."

Mrs. William stood there and only shook her head for a few seconds. *Am I not getting through to them at all?* "Alright, I'll cut this talk short…"

More cheers.

"Ah, huh. School is nearly done for the day. I'm sure you boys and girls can't wait to play Panday on your Gameboys or watch the movies for the hundredth time…?"

[Laughter].

"You are dismissed, students."

Magazine articles worldwide and various TV talk shows and radio broadcasts asked the question: Are the Panday films dangerous and do they pose a problem for the younger generation?

On Oprah's show, she asked the same question to a panel of sociologists and behaviorists, experts in psychology and a Catholic priest. They said:

"The Panday problem does not exist for young people. They embrace the films. The boys *are* Panday! Even the girls. They relate to Ang's struggles to survive in a hard, changing world. Oppressed, forced into slavery is something people, especially children, can relate to. The Panday problem is *our* problem, not the problem of youth."

"I don't see how you can say that. Of course, the movies have taken the world by storm. But there are young people outraged by the violence and that's wonderful to know and see. Everyone hasn't fallen for Panday. I have faith that what filmmakers and promoters have produced will be exposed for what the films are:

TS Caladan

Profit-Machines that appeal to the blood-thirsty in our human nature and not anything good and pure."

"I can't agree with that. The young who oppose Panday have no voice. Their words are drowned out by all the glitz and wild promo ads, which are everywhere these days. On YouTube videos, in ads on the side of websites, everywhere! It's pushed! That's the problem. Panday has taken over. And I don't agree that audiences will come to their senses and realize they're promoting blood and violence and will stop watching. Panday has only grown to incredible proportions and I don't think there's any stopping it."

"But are the films really making people violent? What cases are there in the newspaper that my son or daughter has gotten hurt playing Panday, like it's a _____ game!? I haven't seen or heard anything like that."

"I agree. Where is direct evidence that Panday has caused damage or hurt anyone? We know of nothing like that, people."

"That does not mean violence hasn't occurred; maybe we simply have not heard of those stories on purpose?"

The priest said: "The planet has been in a terrible state lately. The queen warned everyone that 'Darkness will consume the Light.' Sin is all around us and accepted as normal behavior. And into the mix, we now add the phenomenon of Panday. It has blinded the children, and I must say, that was probably its intention from the very beginning. I agree that the problem is its massive promotion machine and, yes, there's no signs of it slowing down. Producers profit on blood. *Vengeance,* Eye-for-an Eye, is nothing new in films. *Hang 'em High, Seventh Samauri*...vengeance might be at the core of

~42~

95% of all movies! Nothing new. But Panday and the global mania that's pushed around it just, just takes this genre to a whole new, bloody level never seen before. Of course it hurts society."

Oprah told the audience: "And we'll be back."

In another country (Mongolia), father Pam said to mother Noko in their living room and in their own language: "Too much violence. Children should never watch. How many Panday films are there now? 6? Or are there 7?"

Noko replied, "I was caught up in Panday-mania, like the rest. I closely followed the series until 3. That's when I knew: *this is wrong!* Children, swords, blood, and we see it graphically displayed? I was wrong for letting our children watch. Six films. The last one was released two months ago, number 6."

Pam had his phone and received a different answer from Google. "No, there's 7. Says *Edge of the Sword* or Panday 7 was released this March, 3 months ago…"

"What?! That's *impossible*. I followed the series closely and you haven't. I've never heard of Edge of the Sword!"

"Look for yourself." He handed the phone to her.

Noko's eyes enlarged and her mouth dropped. "No." I'll check another site. …No! What? Can't be. Edge of the Sword?"

Pam suggested, "Noko. You missed it. That's all."

"Oh no, I didn't." She was very certain. "Last one in the series was *Panday – Unification* and it came out two months ago. I'll look up Unification, huh? Ah, no, no, no…that's not right!"

"What's it say?"

Noko answered, "According to this: Unification was released last year! Last year? I hated Unification, but I know when I saw it, and that was some months ago. Not last year." She shook her head and then looked into her husband's eyes. She said, "Has the world twisted the truth, or is my memory shot to hell?"

"Here's tea, dear."

You wouldn't think Panday Fight Clubs would exist (like secret raves), but PFCs exist in a few states and in a few countries. Linked through the Internet. The boys trained in rings like K-2 matches in the Budokan. The swords were not razor-sharp where they sliced and killed. Swords PFCs used were blunted on the edge. They were extremely dangerous; players maimed other players. Although, deaths were reported. News of the existence of PFCs and deaths associated with them, did not tarnish or lessen Panday enthusiasts. Panday only got bigger and bigger.

It was as if the entire Earth changed. The strange change that *only a few people even noticed,* was felt…everywhere. The world was darker now. Deadly. Children weren't safe. People weren't safe anymore. That was the sense of things, as if a negative vibration was in the air and in the ground. It was collectively *felt.* The planet had turned into a *madhouse* and "we're all mad here." Nothing worked as it did. There were computer glitches, much more than ever before! Machines did not function smoothly, as they had. It seemed as if there was always something wrong! Something almost unfixable and something people never had to deal with in the past.

What changed? What caused awesome *dread,* this

useless feeling now buried in people's hearts and souls? The sense was: No one cared anymore. People were very heartless, soulless and lost the last bits of morality and compassion. They were the Walking Dead. Why live in a world this terrible and meaningless? Then reality changed even more:

September 2020

MON	TUES	WED	THUR	FRI	SAT	SUN	PAN
			1	2	3	4	5
6	7	8	9	10	11	12	13
14	15	16	17	18	19	20	21
22	23	24	25	26	27	28	29
30	31						

"Remember, darling. Tomorrow is Panday," Grace reminded Jim, her husband, as she glanced at the calendar in the kitchen.

"It's what-day, tomorrow?"

"You know what day tomorrow is; it's the day we board up the windows! What? You forgot?"

Jim marched into the kitchen, confronted his wife and asked her: "What? What are you talking about?"

Grace said, "Today's September 4th, Sunday. Tomorrow is the 5th, Panday."

"What's Panday? You mean, the movie? You're not making any sense, Grace."

"What's that calendar on the wall tell you?"

He walked closer to it. Then took a second look. Jim ripped it off the wall and laughed. "Ha, ha. You have a joke calendar. Oh, now I get it; this is a promo-calendar from the movie company. Like in the film? The emperor decreed an 8th day of the week, and the 8th day is Panday. Very funny. I guess it's a trick to have people see the movie again on the Pandays, eh? Clever."

Grace didn't know what to say and stood absolutely still for a few moments. All she thought to say was: "Have you lost the last two years of your life, man?! Is this denial? You don't want to face tomorrow, so you pretend the Panday mandate isn't real? Jim?"

It was then that neighbor Mark knocked on the backdoor. Jim opened the door and let him in.

"Mark," Jim said. "Glad to see you. Maybe you can straighten my wife out…?"

"Me?!"

"What's that you got there, buddy?"

Mark said, "The extra shells you wanted me to get you at the Sports store. I'm sure they're the right ones. They are, right?"

"Hey, Mark. I thought you knew me. I hate guns! I don't have a shotgun. I wouldn't allow one in the house!"

Mark nodded, for Jim to turn around.

He turned and saw what was behind him:

Grace had a double-barreled shotgun and stood in the doorway with a mean look on her face. "What were you saying, Jim?"

On the streets of New York, it was a bloodbath. Crazy, insane kids went out on Panday Hell-night! They understood that anyone they saw on the streets would try and kill them. They had to kill the others first. There was a distinct difference in people these days. Society was not like the first *Purge* movies. In Purge movies, people wanted to live, people cared very much to live and fought very hard to survive. That was not the world of today. The youth were willing to throw their lives away. Whether it was overseas in meaningless wars or the madness of meaningless Panday, it was as if the youth didn't care to live anymore. Why not throw it all away because nobody cared?

Los Angeles was a little different on Panday. During the day, snipers were on rooftops and picked off any person on the streets. During the night, large gangs prowled streets and wore certain colors. They were loyal to their gang and their colors. Most cities were this way; you did not want to be outside alone. Rural areas were different, looser: There almost wasn't a Panday on Panday. Many people were fooled and thought Panday was like any other day in the country, but you never knew for sure. People were attacked and killed when they didn't think they would be. In cities, it was all-out war on Hell-Night!

How did the world change into madness, into mob-mentality? Was Panday the spark, the catalyst for all the violence and bloodshed? Many people thought the series of movies caused the Panday mandates, the new laws of legalized murder. They were outraged at the New World. But others accepted Panday, thought it was a good idea and normal to murder approximately 50 days out of the year><.

4
Willy Tonka*

*Story by Roald Doug

Willy Tonka was a Man of Mystery. He was photographed only a few times for magazines and newspapers. He always wore purple pants, a yellow jacket, vest and a yellow top hat. Never interviewed. Willy Tonka lived a very reclusive life, behind a home fortress and an empire of Tonka trucks. Wild stories and odd rumors circulated about the man. He had very few friends and business associates. No family?

Only 5000 Tonka trucks were made a year, far less than any of the competition. Trucks were a huge business because TV ads, computer ads, radio ads, all the ads, were filled to capacity with deals on trucks. Big gas-guzzling trucks whose emissions hurt the planet in the long run. Tonka trucks were safe for the environment. They didn't hurt the planet because they were electric, the finest electric vehicles on the road! One push of a button and a quiet hush of the engine. There were amazing innovations, more than a Tucker, and too numerous to mention. But what made the Tonka T-Rex a masterpiece in design and engineering was its tremendous performance on every level. Super-craftsmanship, astounding and unmatched. Precision-made, tough road-machines. Quality trucks at a time of very expensive, low-quality trucks. "Most powerful electric vehicle ever!" The ads did not exaggerate or lie like other commercials did. The trucks got incredible mileage before the next recharge and the T-Rex was super-fast. The shocker was the price! Other companies would have charged $100,000 for the same truck, but they could never build one close to a Tonka. Willy's corporation manufactured the greatest truck of all time and brought the price under $20,000. The vehicles were thought to have been "made by Magic." No car/truck company could produce an all-terrain vehicle of such super quality and low price. Tonka only made 1000 red trucks, 1000 blue trucks, 1000 black trucks, 1000 white trucks and 1000 yellow trucks a year! That's all.

Willy's favorite color was yellow, the color of his suit and hat and also the color of his favorite Tonka truck.

True stories circulated about Willy. Stories such as: if you had the money for a Tonka truck, that did not mean you could buy one. Willy, Man of Mystery, investigated every client that wanted a Tonka. If he didn't like you; if you were a horrible person and cheated people, stepped on people to get where you are? Sorry, friend. No Tonka. Jay Leno could not get one. It was up to Mr. Tonka to decide whether you were worthy enough to own a Tonka.

Rumors were true. Plenty of C.E.O.s, politicians and celebrities were refused ownership; they couldn't buy a Tonka no matter how much money they offered.

Tonka trucks were the most sought-after vehicles, ever! No one had ever seen such trucks before. People wanted a Tonka truck more than they wanted a DeLorean, Jaguar, Lamborghini, Maserati or Rolls Royce or any car you can imagine! Posters were made of: "Tonka Truck Dreams," *a vehicle you'll never own.*

Then came the Contest:

The company/corporation (Willy) was giving away a free yellow truck, but much/much more: One person could win a job at the factory as general manager of their own division of Tonka trucks and be Willy Tonka's right-hand man or woman! The job came with a salary of a million dollars a year! But more than that: To be let into the secret Tonka Factory-works! Where all the Magic happened! To know how the trucks were actually produced and see the MAGIC firsthand~ **Wow**! That was the real prize. Willy offered a 49% share of the total company to the winner of the Contest. This made headlines and front pages of newspapers around the country. Everyone was buzzed with the news. The exclusive truck was nothing – it was the *magic* within factory walls that was the real treasure, plus 49% of Tonka Trucks!

RULES OF THE CONTEST [statement given to the press]:

"One person must purchase a brand new, yellow, Tonka truck. They must check the dashboard's rearview mirror, open it. If nothing is found inside, you are not a winner. But you have purchased a lovely truck like no other truck in the world. If you have unscrewed the mirror and discovered the truck's Yellow Slip (not pink slip) inside, then you are a possible winner. Out of the 1000 yellow trucks made this year, THREE of them will contain the hidden Yellow Slips. Once the 3 potential winners are rounded up, they and only they, will have an exclusive tour of Tonkaland secret production facilities in Topeka. Three people will know factory-secrets and see unbelievable sights never dreamed before! They will discover exactly how the beautiful trucks, like perfect gems, are built...and they will be amazed. But there will be only one winner. Mr. Wonka plans to test the winners vigorously, to guarantee he has made the right choices. He leaves it up to the serendipity of the universe to choose 3. But only Willy Tonka decides the ultimate winner and person that will co-own the company. As always, Mr. Tonka reserves the right to not sell you a truck."

At the home of the Sandersons, in Poughkeepsie, New York, the matriarch (Sam) called a family gathering together. After a fine stew dinner, the Sandersons placed chairs in a circle, as Sam directed them to do. He had an important speech prepared that everyone but Billy was aware of. Once the room settled, grampa spoke to his sweet and loving family:

"Okay. You know darn well I've been busting to tell y'all and some of you, if not all, have jumped the gun and already know. *Dammit,* I wanted it to be a surprise to the women, Auntie Ruth, and the little ones. But everyone, ha, already seems to know...ha..."

"Know what, grandpa?" Billy asked.

"Except Billy. But that's Okay 'cos it will be the biggest surprise to him. Now, boy, I have a hypothetical for you. If you had, oh, say, 20 thousand dollars in your hands, huh. Tell me. What would you do with it?"

"That's easy! I'd buy me a Tonka truck and enter the big Contest. I wanna see how they build one, *you know that!*" Billy said with excitement and joy in his heart.

Grampa Sanderson asked, "About, ah, how many times have you told us your dream? One where you see yourself driving a T-Rex?"

"About a hundred times, I guess." Billy replied.

The men and a few of the women knew what grampa had up his sleeve and wanted to see the look on Billy's face. They all smiled.

"Then, here!" The old guy tossed a small bag on Billy's lap. It contained $20,000 cash!

"Grampa! Did you rob a bank for me?!"

"No, no, ha. Nothing like that, boy."

"Then, how?"

"We'll let your mother hang onto the bag. It's yours, all yours, believe me. And your uncle John and Frank pitched in a few thousand. You should thank them."

The young man ran over to them and hugged them.

"Our pleasure, Billy."

"Let's just see that you win now, eh?"

He turned to his grandfather and asked again: "But, how did you get it?"

"Ha. Your mother knows. And certainly, your grandmother knew, God rest her soul. I was a very lucky lad back in the old country when I was young, about your age. Only your hair is blonder, ha. There was a town lottery and I won. I had some battles to keep it, but I won those fights and kep it. *Ten thousand dollars* when I came over here and transferred it to dollars. It's grown over time. With your uncles' help, we made it $20,000 and we sure know what yer gonna do with it…"

Suddenly a loud KNOCK at the door!

"Put the money away." The bag was hidden behind the couch.

"Awfully loud. I'll get it," Billy's mother Mabel said. She opened the door and was slightly startled at the tall, dark, thin figure at the door. He wore a large, black top hat. He was bald, had pale skin and had spooky eyes, shaved off brows.

"May I come in? This concerns your son, mam," he said in a deep, slow voice.

"My son?" Mabel was surprised and let the stranger in.

Everyone in the room was surprised. The men got to their feet. John asked, "And you are?"

He said: "I am Mr. Snide…"

"Snide?"

"Yes, Snide. I have a few questions for Billy Sanderson. Is that the boy, there?" Snide's eyes got larger.

"Wait."

"Just a minute, sir. Who are you?" Frank asked.

"Mr. Tonka sent me…"

"Willy Tonka!" Billy yelled and smiled a big smile.

"Well, Okay. Why don't you sit right here, Mr. Snide," Mabel suggested. "Would you like some tea?"

"It's not 4PM, so, no." The odd man's eyes jerked from side to side as if someone was over his shoulder. "Are you ready, young man?"

"Sure. I do well on tests. Shoot."

Snide asked, "Have you been in jail, and if so, how long were you incarcerated?"

"He's 17 years old! Just got his learner's permit to

drive. He never leaves the house. What the hell kinda trouble he's gonna get into?!"

"Grandpa. Let me answer. Mr. Tonka wants to know these things. No, I have never been in jail."

"Question two. Are you a virgin?"

"See here!" John yelled.

Frank, the lawyer, said, "That's inappropriate and irrelevant! Don't answer that, Billy."

Mabel mouthed the same question to him, silently.

Billy was confused, shook his head and shrugged.

"Last question," Mister Snide said.

Frank Sanderson said, "Hold on. Nothing makes sense here. Are we all forgetting something?"

"What?"

"Mr. Snide. Something's very fishy in Poughkeepsie. How do you know Billy's going to buy a yellow Tonka and be in the contest?"

"Hey, that's right."

"Yeah."

"We just surprised Billy with the idea of it tonight. And you're at our door with questions from Willy Tonka?"

Mabel crossed her arms. "Can you explain that, Mr. Snide? It's not like he's already bought it. It's not like he found the Yellow Slip in the mirror. We're only now able to buy it. How do you know to be here and do you investigate every person thinking about entering the Contest? That's about a million people, Santa Claus, how you gonna do that?"

"Yeah."

Grampa offered an answer: "Maybe, just maybe, Tonka is psychic and it's fate, eh? He's like Kreskin and he knows Billy's gonna win!" The old man turned to

Billy with big eyes and declared "Yer gonna win, Billy! This, this, strange man is a good sign…"

"Third question! If you won the ultimate prize, Billy…"

"Yes?"

Snide asked the boy, seriously: "Would you be strong enough to give everything you've won AWAY to another person…and leave the Tonka factory with absolutely nothing?"

"Ah."

"That's such an unfair question, Mr. Snide," Frank said.

"Nevertheless, it's the final question. Tell you wot? Mull it over in your brain a while, Billy. But the decision has to be yours and yours alone. When you get to the factory, I mean, *if* you get to the factory, the third question will be asked of you by me one more time…so, think it over. *Good-night."* He tipped his black hat and smiled, which was a surprise since his expression was very morose and somber, the whole time. Mr. Snide, who appeared as a funeral director, was gone.

"What do you think, grandpa?"

"Ha, ha! I think you'll be one of the winners! And have the same Scottish luck that I had long ago! Yay! Let's dance."

The Sandersons were very happy. They put on music, grabbed one another and danced.

Billy, Sam (gramps) and Mabel were at the Tonka dealership where 5 yellow trucks were displayed with bright spotlights on them. The Sandersons were thrilled to see the trucks, the logos and the massive showroom! The threesome marched up to one of the salesmen in a nice, yellow suit. The purchase was made immediately, but only after cameras were trained on them. Willy Tonka remotely approved and they were green-lighted. Funds were transferred and one of the 5 identical model T-Rexs belonged to Billy Sanderson. His 17-year-old status was *raised* to 18 so he could be the sole owner of a Tonka truck. All Billy had to do was pick one, which might take time and a lot of thought.

The salesman told them: "We had 10 yellow ones in the beginning and only 5 are left. The choice is yours, young man."

"That one." It didn't take much time at all. Billy knew. Billy drove it home and he was incredibly happy.

The yellow Tonka T-Rex sped home fast, and screeched into the driveway! Mabel, Sam and Billy were greeted by a group of family members and neighbors. *They cheered* and hoped with all their hearts that Billy found a Yellow Slip. Gramps, Mabel and Billy clutched the mirror with all their might and *broke it off.* They brought it out into the light, on the grass. Uncle John had a screwdriver ready. While a few others held the mirror and extension down firm, John unscrewed the mirror from the setting just like contest instructions said. It came loose and he tossed the mirror on the grass. They looked inside. They all looked inside. There was nothing there. Nothing. "Aw." "I was so sure." "It's gonna break his..." "Damn."

Billy looked down into the fixture and also saw that nothing was in the mirror-shaped impression. No Yellow Slip. The whole gang felt terrible for the boy.

"So sad."

"I wonder how many families did the same thing we

did?"

"It'll be 997."

"I'm sorry, Billy."

Billy Sanderson picked up the mirror from the lawn. He was going to fix the mirror and thought about how to reattach it, when he felt something on the other side. When he turned it over, he saw a folded, taped slip of paper. *It was yellow!* "Aaaaugh!! Look!" he unfolded it and waved it for friends and family~.

The crowd screamed!

Mabel cried.

Frank and John high-fived!

Grampa Sam danced the jig!

It was true: Billy Sanderson was one of three Tonka Contest winners who had a chance to be set for life and really help out his very good, kind and generous family.

The news was announced on television and in newspapers. The winners were Billy Sanderson, 18-year-old from Poughkeepsie, NY. Jennifer Seether, 21-year-old from Wheeling, W.VA. and Wayne Shaddish, 55-year-old from Encino, CA. The date arrived and the opening of the factory's front door was an incredible, high-profile event in Topeka, Kansas. Four TV networks were there, a lot of local news people and unexpected celebrities were in attendance just to see Willy Tonka out in public. (Never happened). Above the truck factory flew two helicopters. Today's gate-opening was a big deal.

Then, it happened. The long/iron gate creaked open, slowly. Out shot a very small version of Willy's yellow "Model-T-Rex," one third the size. Willy just fit in the tiny driver's seat. He was excited; he waved, smiled and laughed in front of a few thousand people. Cameras and phones clicked away. Tonka and a large crowd might never happen again. He stepped out of the mini-truck.

Tonka was in the usual outfit that he wore in his press photos: purple pants, yellow jacket, vest and a yellow top hat. Willy added a cane and swung it with flair from side to side. The crowd loved it and cheered. Then he spoke to them:

"I want to thank you all for this swell moment; I'm choked up, friends." He touched a place on his body that was not his heart. "I have been looking forward to this day, and by the end of the day, we will have the ultimate winner of the contest, the person I will hand the Keys to my Kingdom over to!"

Cheers!

"Now I want the 3 people with the Yellow Slips to come forward. Step up; there's only three of you. There you are…and you are?"

"I'm Jennifer Seether and here's my slip. Ha, ha." She turned to one of the cameras to get her good side.

"I'll take that." Willy grabbed it, hard. Jennifer barely noticed him. Her attention was on the camera.

"Go. You go, that way."

She walked off, waved to the crowd as if she was a famous model.

"Next, you are?"

"William Sanderson, sir. They call me Billy. I wanted to tell you, this is a dream come true for me, sir, and…"

Willy interrupted the young man and said, "Well, the day is young and I am not…so, over there you go. Now, last one. Okay, this is the old guy, right?"

"I'm 55, Mr. Tonka. That's old?" the man joked and smiled. "Wayne Shaddish, at your service! I do bathrooms. If you need new bathrooms, I can give you the best deal. Here's my card..."

"Right." Tonka seemed bored and swished his cane in front of the man in a gray suit. "Over there, over there. I want you all to get on the Tonkavator, I call it a Tonkavator."

The three of them got in back of the mini-truck that was suddenly – larger? There was only Willy's small seat. *Now, there were three additional seats behind the driver's seat and the whole vehicle appeared considerably larger than it was.*

"Weird," Miss Seether said.

They got in and '80s music played from the yellow truck. Truck turned and went back in through the gate. A lot of waves and cheers.

Willy Tonka stood up. He felt elated and confessed: "I never had a family. It's like I have a family! Isn't it great!?" He waved the cane in circles and almost hit the passengers. Then, he gunned the vehicle>>.

The Tonkavator suddenly sped at very high speed toward the heart of the factory. Background things were bright and showed strange tubes, tunnels, girders and sprockets of bright colors. The vehicle went faster and faster. The passengers were scared. Just before Billy came close to being tossed out of the seat...

The Tonkavator truck stopped smoothly, turned on its thick/rubber wheels and sped to a wall, bright pink in color. Now, *the truck moved up the wall, vertically, very fast!* The seats turned so Willy and his passengers had perfect views of the factory floor from a high, bird's eye view. The Tonkavator stopped, the seats jerked, but everyone was alright. Oingo Boingo music ended ['Dead Man's Party'].

"Look at me now, people. You have to sign a document; it's just a formality, an agreement. If you don't, you can't go any farther and you must leave now…" Willy gave each one a yellow piece of paper.

"What?"

Wayne stated, "I never sign something I haven't read…"

Tonka insisted: "You can read it. Read it."

Jennifer said, "I'll sign." She signed with a big, feathered pen.

"Me, too," Billy said and signed his paper.

Mr. Shaddish asked, "What's that fine print down there, Tonka?"

He replied, "There has to be fine print or it's not official…"

"I'm not signing!" Wayne replied. "No way."

Tonka told him: "If you don't sign, Mr. Shaddish, you forfeit everything, even your lovely T-Rex…"

"Okay, I'll sign." The feather tickled his nose.

"Okay, people. Now you can take a good gander at our factory."

"Wow," Billy expressed. "This is where you build trucks?"

"No, Billy. Those tracks, ramps and curly-Qs are where we test them! Race them. Play with them. To all of you, I take it you never really opened up your Model-T-Rex to turbo-mode, aye? To see how fast she can go?"

Wayne replied, "Mr. Tonka. I've taken my Rex on the autobahn to test that very question: what's its top speed? Zero to 150 in 5 seconds. For an all-terrain vehicle, I got it to 150 MPH and that is incredible! I salute you, sir. You know no truck goes that fast. Amazing. I don't know what turbo means, but I know

150 is the Rex's top speed…"

Willy asked, "Mr. Shaddish. Would you believe its top speed is 300 miles per hour!? Do you believe that?"

"I don't believe that, Mr. Tonka."

Willy looked into the eyes of the passengers as they were perched high over the Tonka test area. All eyes buzzed as if he would drive them 300 MPH. And he did!

The Tonkavator (small version of the Model-T, with extra seats) slid down the walls and accelerated as soon as it hit the floor. BAM, OFF LIKE A LIGHTNING BOLT! Willy said, "Hang on! You don't want to fall out going 300 miles an hour!" The vehicle hit the long straightaway and went faster and faster!

"No seatbelts?" Jennifer exclaimed and held on for dear life.

Tonka laughed, "Seatbelts! Ha, ha, ha, ha! They're for suckers!"

Billy told Jennifer, "The Rex Model-Tonka doesn't have seatbelts, didn't you see? That's because they're not needed. You are perfectly safe inside a Tonka, isn't that right, sir?"

"Kid, you are such a suck-up, I can't believe it," Tonka joked.

Jennifer and Wayne laughed. So did Billy.

"But we're not inside a Model-T, it's a Tonkavator and *we're not inside anything; we're barely hanging on! Faster! Faster!"* The mini-truck with extra seats hit 200 MPH, then 250 and then 300! Suddenly, the straight track came to an end. Something was out ahead and blocked the path. Willy slammed on the 'Automatic Quick-Break in 5 seconds' and screamed to his passengers: "Don't hold on! Don't hold on! Let go! Let go!" He knocked Billy's hand so that it was free…

The Tonkavator STOPPED. Stopped so dramatically that all four were thrown right out in front of them and landed on what seemed like a very large and very soft, yellow cloud. It was a big pillow designed to catch the passengers at the end of the track.

"No worries. Happens everyday in Tonkaland," Willy told the three winners.

"Aah! You might have warned us, Mr. Tonka! I'm not as young as I used to be. I could have been killed! Or had a heart attack or hurt?"

"No, no," Willy replied casually. "Sue me, then. No, no. If you'd have held on, you'd've been hurt. That's why I told ya to let go. Perfectly safe ride. Let's move on."

Billy picked up Jennifer. She appreciated his help. They shared a warm moment. Billy knew she was older, but she was a real cute brunette. They traded smiles.

"This way." He pointed his cane. Tonka took them to a yellow "moving sidewalk," which led in a different direction from the track.

"Cool."

"Don't you have moving sidewalks out there? Where you live?" Willy honestly asked. He didn't know.

"No, sir. We don't."

Like a child with big blue eyes, Willy said, "Well, you should."

It was then that Willy wanted to cheer them up and himself. He also wanted to give them something to think about. So, he sang:

"Come with me, and you'll be, in a world of pure imagination. We'll begin, truck spin, in a world of my creation. What you'll see, will defy…explanation.

If you want to view paradise, simply look around and view it. Anything you want to do, do it. Wanna change the world...there's nothing to it.

There is no life I know, to compare, with pure imagination. Living there, you'll be free...if you truly wish to be."

"That was divine, Mr. Tonka. You sing like a bird," Wayne said.

Billy smiled and expressed: "Magical."

Jennifer had an attitude. "I'm a good singer too, you know?"

Tonka said, "I'm sure you are, young lady. But others should say that, not you. I should say, my most precious secrets are just ahead. Part of the contract, Mr. Shaddish, is how you *cannot* divulge any of my secrets to anyone! Hope that is perfectly clear, people? I do not want the public to know the truth about my trucks. I want MYSTERY. You signed a nondisclosure agreement, that's all."

"Okay."

"Oh, look there, young people and sir. Now, you will soon be inside the heart of Tonkaland. Get ready! You will see one of the Big Secrets. How the Model-T-Rex trucks, which are gemstones! How, with fine-precision of German watches, the trucks *are made.* Formed, sculpted into creation, like Michaelangelo created the Mona Lisa..."

"Excuse me, Mr. Tonka," Billy interrupted. "...But Leonardo di Vinci painted the Mona Lisa..."

"Ha! Funny, I thought he painted the church ceiling. Ha. Switch it! As I was not saying yet, but will say now: one Big Secret of Tonkaland is not *how* the trucks are made…it is…are you ready? It is WHO is making them! Bet you'll be surprised when you see the little buggers that actually build the trucks. We're coming to the factory itself right now. Jump off the walkway; we can walk the rest of the way. Ah, *there they are* (smiled) and it's so weird that they happen to be in my favorite color…"

"What the hell?" Billy saw them first and reacted.

"Language!" Tonka yelled a bit.

"Funny, little men, ha," Jennifer said and giggled.

"They're Loompa Oompas…"

The yellow men were chubby and no more than 4-feet high. They had short arms. Twenty of them were in white jumpsuits and appeared very, very happy. They synchronize-danced around parts slowly, but perfectly, as they built a truck.

Shaddish asked, "Loompa whatas?"

"I rescued them from a cruel, tyrant God-King in the jungles of Borneo; I was on vacation. Loompa Oompas are intelligent craftsmen. It's like they have a secret language between them. I know that because they do. I brought 'em around to my place in Topeka and they got hooked on TV. Not the shows…*truck commercials!* Their leader, Benji, looked me right in the face and squarely said, 'We can build better trucks.' I believed the kid. With my inheritance money, I created TONKA. But the little fellas actually build 'em. Hell, I wasn't even into trucks until the Loompa Oompas came along, ha."

"That's an incredible story, Mr. Tonka," Wayne commented.

Billy said, "Wow."

"We appreciate the privilege of finding out about your secrets, Mr. Tonka," Jennifer Seether said. With a sly smile, she added: "There's probably zillions of news agencies, talk shows or TMZ that'll pay a fortune for your secrets…"

"That's for sure," Willy Tonka agreed and noticed *temptation* in Jennifer's heart, that if she didn't win the 'ultimate prize,' she might~.

"Oh, you're in luck, people. It's time for one of their songs."

They all sang: *"Loompa Oompa do padi do. I have another puzzle for you. Loompa Oompa do padi dee. If you are wise, you'll listen to me. Loompa Oompa do padi da. If you're not spoiled, you will go far. You will live in happiness too. Like the Loompa Oompa do padi do!"*

"Shocking, to say the least. And they turn out 5000 of these babies per year?" Wayne asked a question and he knew the answer.

"Yes, sir," Willy replied and smiled with pride. "But we have more rides and chills and spills to experience for sure! Much more! This way! Back on the moving sidewalk."

The foursome jumped on the yellow track and steadily went back the way they came.

Billy asked Willy, "May I ask you a personal question, sir?"

"Of course! Ask away, Billy! I have nothing to hide. Ha, ha, ha, ha. Didja hear what I said? Nuttin' to hide. Gee wilikers."

"I was curious about your family, sir. You said you didn't have a family. That's hard for me to grasp. I am extremely close to mother, Auntie Ruth, my uncles. And especially, grandpa. I have the greatest family in the world…"

"What about your father, Billy? Where's he?"

"I thought I was asking the personal questions, sir?"

There was a glint in Willy's eye and a tear in Billy's.

Billy confessed, "My father is an unknown factor. He ran away, skipped out on all of us. I never knew him." Billy's head looked up. "But I know the importance of family. Sorry, ah, to hear about…"

"Water under the bridge! Forget the past! What's important is NOW! And now, or soon, you will witness and experience my crowning achievement! Oh, shit, POOP, I shouldn't have sworn. It's *the Loompas* crowning achievement, Okay? Okay? *Don't you tell anyone!*" He swished the cane a few more times. "Heck, I just sit back and marvel at what they'll come up with next. You are going to have the thrill of your lives in the T-2!! The Rex-2!! Can you imagine in your wildest dreams what the Model-Rex 2 can do??"

"Rex-2?"

"We're gonna ride in the Rex-2?" Wayne said and he didn't know what he said.

"This is my Biggest Secret and, believe it or not…it's the Future! We will take a spin in a **Super Truck from the Future.** I feel like singing again:

"There is no life, I know, to compare with pure imagination. There's no time, but today, for prestidigitation. To fly free, and be, beyond all that you can see. Dreams come true…if you truly wish them to."

"Nice."

"Is that it, Mr. Tonka? The T-2!" Billy was excited when he turned his head and saw the new model. Yellow, of course. He held onto Jennifer and she didn't mind.

Willy Tonka was extremely serious for a few seconds. He didn't joke. He whispered into Billy's ear, "We are the music-makers. We are the movie-makers. We are the dreamers of dreams."

The message was too much for young Billy, who had his eyes glued to the Rex-2.

They all jumped off the walkway and ran to the vehicle.

Loompa Oompas were in the background and showed off their great Truck-Art (with arm gestures) like they were models that presented what you might win on a gameshow. Then, they left.

"It's a truck-spaceship! It flies through space?" Billy screamed.

"I asked the Loompas about that. They said they're reserving space travel for the Rex-3."

"Oh. OH!"

Jennifer laughed.

Get in!" Willy instructed.

They all did and found ultra-comfortable seats – the perfect 4-seater. When the starter button was depressed, you heard nothing. Not the slightest hum, but the Rex-2 was ready to be a rocket, and it did! **Blast!** Vooooooooom! The wheels retracted (they were only used as legs when the Rex-2 was grounded). The new model truck was a hovercraft that skimmed over the surface at very high velocities!

"Now, let's take that straightaway we took before in this baby!" Tonka yelled. His passengers were more excited than they were before. "Yeah!!" "Yes!!"

It was the most bizarre sensation inside the new model. Seat belts were not needed because there was no sense of movement inside the Rex-2, like it was *magic*. But outside the windows, Tonkaland was seen whipping by at incredible speeds. Faster and faster and faster!!!

Willy Tonka sang once more, but it wasn't a soft, beautiful melody…it was in a scary, nightmarish voice…

"There's no way of knowing, which direction we are going! There's no way of knowing, the way we are rowing! Or which way the river's flowing! And there's no sign of us ever slowing!!"

Directly ahead of the T-2 in "rocket-mode," was one of the curly-Q formations, also called "loopty-loop." Model-Rex trucks sped along the track, went up and around and were flung high into the air, but always safely landed on thick (magnetic) tires! The Rex-2 was going to do something entirely different…

When the rocket-Tonka flew fast over the track and did the loop, it also jettisoned high up into the air at a very fast rate of speed. Then **it FLEW on its own!** T-2 had powerful jets that kept it over the ground and made it maneuver like a controlled bullet!

"Weeeeeeeeeeeeeeeeeeee!!!!" Wayne exclaimed, then said: "But it's like we're not moving! Fantastic!"

Jennifer said to Billy, "Smooth. I love it."

"I never dreamed…*flying*. Wow." Billy said in awe.

The foursome was thrilled at the sights when they looked below. *They flew over cheering crowds in Topeka, Kansas!* Large crowds were still camped and huddled around Tonkaland this special day. It was only Topeka, Kansas, but the super view was from the clouds!

"Surprised the hell out of me, oh sorry, that the Loompas got a truck to fly! I'll never doubt Benji again!

Haaa!" Willy told them.

They waved to the people below and the people waved back. Especially happy were the Sandersons; they cheered much harder when they recognized Billy's head out of Rex-2's window. It was a grand day! [But the day was not over].

Willy pushed a button and the Rex turned green in color. Green? Another button made it blue, then orange, then purple, then red.

Tonka sang again:

"Come with me, and you'll see, magic in all of its perfection. Beauty and joy of invention. Steering in every direction. ...Come with me, and you'll see...paradise."

"Aw."

Billy asked, "Now what, Mr. Tonka?"

"Now...we come down to Earth." It was as if Willy Tonka changed from a friendly mood, into a *not-so-friendly mood*. "You 3 must talk to Mr. Snide. You know, the thin/creepy man in black, with a top hat. I swear he got the top hat idea from me..."

"Snide?"

"Oh, I remember Mister Snide," Mr. Shaddish said. "Scared the *hell* out of me, I mean, the piss out of me, aah!"

"Me, too," Jennifer said.

Tonka said, "Now, don't be frightened, young people and sir, when I push the yellow button and exit the vehicle. It was the Loompas' cool way of getting out of the Rex-2. No hands. It's been programmed to go back into the factory on its own." Willy said in a mean tone: "You will be let off at Mr. Snide's office; he awaits you for the final question! Our business has concluded! Good day to you all!!" Tonka pushed the yellow button hard…and he *disappeared!*

"Gone? Gee. Well, that's odd for him to say and cop an attitude. We were having such a good time," Wayne expressed, as the aircraft slipped down and flew over the factory floor.

"I don't believe it. What test, what questions?" Jennifer said. Snide did not ask her the pre-questions, only announced: she might be the ultimate winner, which whetted her desire to win the Contest.

Billy was the one who was the most concerned: *Why would Mr. Tonka change and go from magical to almost maniacal? And turn on them? Did he know the future? Will each of the three winners fail him and not be worthy of being the Ultimate Winner?* he thought. Billy's whole family wanted his happiness most of all, and the young man knew that. He didn't want to disappoint them; he wanted very much to help them since they had sacrificed a lot. *Maybe I won't get the final question right?* Worry was written all over his face. Then…

Jennifer touched his hand. She read his face and hugged him.

Billy realized that: If he did not win it all, he might still have a relationship with Jennifer? Possibly. Unless. Unless she was the big winner, then she'd have nothing to do with him, of course.

The red Rex-2 stopped right outside the dark, dreary office of Mr. Snide. The three were directed into a black waiting room. Then each one was brought separately into the black office.

The shocker was that a public statement by Mister Tonka was released over all Media channels and networks: It stated that *none of the three Slip holders qualified for the Ultimate Prize!* As stipulated in the rules of the Contest. Because of the three failures, **they forfeited everything and even lost the ownership of their Model-Rex truck!**

The outcry by the crowd and the worldwide audience was swift and strong: They criticized Willy Tonka as a fraud, a liar, a charlatan, a capitalist and "swindler of people's dreams!" He was now hated.

Billy and Jennifer were shattered at the news, even though Jen had not been questioned by Mr. Snide as yet. They hugged and cried.

Tonka realized he'd have to speak to the public and once again, the large/iron gate of Tonkaland opened...but, only opened a little bit.

He attempted an explanation...

Old Grandpa Sanderson was front and center and *tackled Tonka before he spoke a word.* The gate automatically closed and almost trapped a person.

Sam got up off the ground and yelled: "What kinda person are you, Tonka?! Destroying a boy's dreams like that!? What was it all about, this charade, this lie?!" Sam was certain Billy would win and be the Ultimate Winner. 100% positive; he felt it deep inside his Scottish bones! "It can't be! All the build-up and tease, and then have No Winner!?" Grandpa wanted to kill the man in yellow and purple.

Instead of Willy being sorry in the least, he doubled down! He got angrier than grandpa Sam! "They signed the contract and it clearly stated, not so clearly stated, switch that. But LEGALLY stated that they lose everything if they miss the 3rd Question asked by Mr. Snide! According to Mr. Snide, the first two did! You get nothing!!'"

Sam said, "You made a truck fly, Mr. Tonka! You can do anything!! You can't hurt my grandchild like that, after you built him up. Damn you!!" He shook his boney fist.

"Okay, Okay. Sorry to disappoint you, grandpa, but the fact is I would never be permitted to market my new model that flies. They're for demonstration only. *You think that doesn't burn my butt?!* I'd love to really, really change the world. I can't. But if I can steer the next generation, then maybe, possibly, hopefully, maybe they can? For the better, you know what I'm saying, pops?"

Sam said, "So, that's it then? The boy didn't win?"

"Ah, maybe there is a tiny spark of a chance, aye? A wee, wee, micro, slim, hardly a hair of a chance – but it'll never happen. Never."

"What?"

"I jumped the gun with my announcement to the Press. Mr. Shaddish missed the question and Billy missed the question. Jennifer is being interviewed as we speak in one damn long interview! We know her greedy little heart: she thinks she's a princess, that she's entitled to everything! She's not going to get the third question right!"

"Hey, what's that?" grampa asked when he saw a strange creature that walked toward them. The little guy was small and yellow.

"That's Benji. He won't eat you."

"For you, sir. A surprise." Benji said, handed Willy a note, then walked off.

"What's this? What's this? Is it true!? Really? I never would have believed it in all my 109 lives!" Willy tossed away his cane. He grabbed Sam and they both danced a jig, around and around.

"What is it? What are you saying, Tonka?"

"She passed, she passed, she passed the third test! I'm so happy. My dream is coming true! Even *my* dreams are coming true there, Sam. Wait till you see! Did you know we're related?"

"What? What are you talking about, Mr. Tonka?"

"I'm your son," Tonka said and his big, blue eyes said it too.

"Albert?"

"I think so. There are tests to prove it now. Ha, ha! Come!" A bright, fiery-red model of the T-2 appeared in a flash, 2 feet over the floor. "Get in. We have a few people to see, aye?"

They got in and the hover-truck sped away, silently.

It quickly arrived at Mr. Snide's black office.

"Stay still for a minute, Sam. You're gonna love this."

Willy pushed a button on the dash and both of them were transported outside of the vehicle and on their feet!

"Gosh." Grampa Sam was amazed and touched himself. He was in one piece.

"Why open a door, right?" Willy said with a smile. "It's for saps."

"Right."

"This way." They entered and saw…

Mister Snide, Jennifer and Billy. Snide was behind a yellow desk, but everything else in the room was black. Billy and Jennifer jumped to their feet. Snide was his cold, lifeless self.

"Grandpa!" Billy was extremely happy to see him and so was Jen.

"Mister Sanderson," she said, with a big smile on her face.

"There's such good news, grandpa!"

"Why, why, what's that? I thought you lost and you, young lady, had no chance of winning? Why are ya happy?"

"What was the third question Mr. Snide asked of Billy when he was in your home, sir?" Willy asked.

"Ah, ah, ha, I ferget at the moment…"

Snide, in his deep voice and with a sullen expression, repeated it:

"Would you be strong enough to give everything you've won AWAY to another person…and leave the Tonka factory with absolutely nothing?"

Tonka said: "Billy thought it was a trick question and answered honestly. He wanted one of my trucks, *badly,* as you know. He thought I would appreciate his honesty and could win that way. But I had to be true to the rules and stipulations in the agreement, right?"

"But I don't get it…" Sam scratched his head and white beard.

"Willy explained, "You see, I had my own dreams, dreams of finding my real father and son. They were kidnapped by a wizard from my planet. I'm not really one of you, if you haven't noticed? I was given a vivid dream that astounded me, probably from the Big Manufacturer in the Sky. And it told me: Have a contest! Put 3 Yellow Slips in mirrors and you'll find your son and a family you've lost! Spells can be put on people, so they forget, or see something that's really not there. Let's just say that my enemy, who I've since defeated, I think, made me *not see* the truth for the longest time. A spell was put on Sam, Mable and your uncles so they didn't recognize me as Albert. I'm Albert Sanderson. The name's not Tonka."

Billy asked, "Your name's not Tonka, Mr. Tonka?"

"No, Billy. Tonka is a Loompa Oompa word for 'pink brother.'"

"Ha, ha."

"Ha. I'll be damned. Sorry."

Billy asked, "Hey, what happened to Mr. Shaddish?"

"He was never there," Tonka said, in a normal tone.

Both Jennifer and Billy were amazed and said: "What?"

"Just a figment, sorry to fake you out. Wayne was a distraction, to have a 3rd element in the mix. The Contest originally announced only two Yellow Slips and only 2 chances to be the Ultimate Winner..."

Billy said, "But there were three?"

"Not any more. History will record only two..."

"But how?"

Willy shook his white gloves and said, "Spells, magic, (sang) *in a world of pure imagination.*"

Grandpa was still very confused and was pretty sure he missed something. Frustrated to understand, he asked, loudly: "But how did Billy WIN!??"

"Ah!" Tonka explained, "Don't you see, Sam? It was so simple. When Jen was asked the question, she said she'd give *everything* to Billy. They're in love. Miss Seether wasn't anything like I thought she was. Inside her soul resides the softness, sensitivity and kindness we all possess...if we dig a little deeper and find it. My dream did not see her do that. I very much hoped she'd give it to Billy and not keep the position, power and wealth for herself. I picked them because they were in my dream, but I didn't know for sure. Ha, ha. *I'm home!*"

Grandpa Sam said, "I'll never get over that you're Albert. I've wondered about him for ages; if he was alright? Funny, funny, funny, how the world works." Sam hugged Albert, Billy and tightly grabbed Jennifer. They were all family now. Or…were they?

"There is one problem that might disturb or destroy this happiness apple-cart, I have to mention. I gotta mention," the man in yellow said. "It could ruin everything, aye?"

"What?!"

"No, no, you mean after all that the kids have been through? Something could still BLOW the deal?!" gramps exclaimed.

"Yes," Tonka said, sadly. It won't be official until the blood test."

"Blood test?"

"That's where Snide comes in. Although, his name's not Mr. Snide, it's Mr. Parkinson. He's a doctor and a lawyer, see?"

When the group looked at the somber man, he had bottles, tubes and apparatus for blood tests on the desk in front of him.

"We have to see for sure, see if my dream was true or not…?"

Sam asked in anger: "What if you're *not* my son!? What if you're not Billy's father?!"

Tonka was devastated by the possibility. "Then all is lost. Then I have not defeated my enemy and the dream was wrong. *No one gets nothing and I am ruined.* So, please. Mr. Parkinson, do your job." He extended his arm. Was Willy Sam's son and Billy's father?? Tests proved that he was! Parkinson beamed from ear to ear; he was happy as a lark! Everyone in the room was! They were all family and welcomed Jennifer into the family as well, Billy's future wife.

"I'm not going to last forever. I need people to carry on my work here at Tonkaland long after I'm gone. I want all of you to live here, in the factory. I'll make extraordinary places for you, you'll see…"

Sam said in amazement: "We could live with you…son?"

"Of course, I don't know if we'll have room for your uncles, the little ones, Auntie Ruth, and your mother, but I'm sure we can fit them all in. Who's going to take care of the Loompas when I'm gone? I need help, gang!"

Hugs and tears and tears and hugs.

Then Albert wondered about Mable. "Mabel. My Mabel…"

"My mother. That's right," Billy said.

"I wonder if she'll remember me, recognize me, now that the Wizard's spell is broken?"

Sam's hand went on his son's shoulder and an arm went around him. He told Albert, "She'll remember you, boy." Tears in their eyes.

Jennifer and Billy kissed.

Then Albert yelled for: "MUSIC!!"

Oingo Boingo's 'Dead Man's Party' *played loudly!*

Everyone danced, especially the Loompa Oompas!

"I'm all dressed up with nowhere to go! Walking with a dead man over my shoulder! Waiting for an invitation to arrive! Going to a party where no one's still alive! I was struck by lightning, walkin' down the street. I was hit by something last night in my sleep. It's a dead man's party, who could ask for more? Everybody's

comin', leave your body and soul at the door! Don't run away! It's only me!"

Happy endings for all. In time, a few big changes were made. They had to be made because Tonkaland was permanently opened to the general public for tours and inspection. No more mysteries. It had to now become a real company with employee wages and benefits and insurances and taxes and accounting, on and on. Jennifer and Billy Tonka changed the company into 'Tonka Enterprises.' The Loompas could not stay as they were, so they were altered, *magically,* into factory workers, humans, who all appeared similar. They were still happy and sang their hearts out. There was less synchronized-dancing.

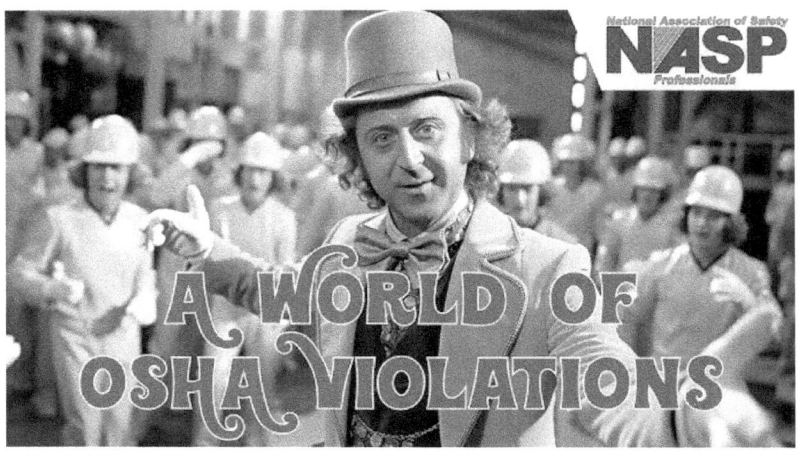

TS Caladan

5
Moon Oblivion

Clone One said to Clone Three, "What the hell's wrong with you, man?"

"What?"

"Didn't they tell you anything? Do you know *nothing* about what you're doing?! The corporation's assignment?"

"Yeah! I know plenty! I know I have to look forward to 3 bloody years with you two jokers! I know that much. I know I bug you, for some reason. Maybe because I look cooler than you? I don't know. Get specific. Now what?!"

"Aren't you supposed to work the worst job, because you're a newbie? That's waste disposal. Two had to do it when he came aboard; I had to do it when I came aboard and your replacement will have to do it too when he replaces you. Get it?"

"Hey, Number One. I've been doing it!"

Clone insisted: "Hardly! The piles are piling up, buddy. So, how about you spending less time calling home when it's the same thing over and over again. Just do your job!"

"I'll get out there, don't worry. In fact, I know my job and my other assignments. I miss home already, Okay? You shouldn't blame me; this is traumatic, you know? What I am not clear on is Two's job assignment and yours. Why don't you inform me what my duties will be when I graduate to the next step, eh? Then, later, I'd love to hear my job when I get to stage 3, and be the veteran of the trio. In other words, what the hell do you do around here except complain?"

One said: "Sure, sure. I have to cut you some slack, kid, because you're new. Like the rest of us, and the people before me, first thing is we miss home, we call home and it's the same damn thing…"

"What do you mean?" Three asked

"Look. I know we clones are different. But when we communicate with Earth, it seems it's always the same story: Our wives have taken the children and moved on. Face it! Three years on the Moon is a tough assignment for anyone, Three. That's a lot to ask for a wife or girlfriend; I know. I'm really trying to help you. I had a hell of a time adjusting. In time…in time, it gets easier. You learn to live with it…"

"Thanks, One. You're not as much of an uptight asshole as I thought you were. Ha."

Three made One laugh. "Ha, ha. I sure appreciate that, Number Three. But the canisters do have to be tossed in the dump, Okay?"

"I swear I will get on it in a minute and dispose of

them all. But let me ask you a few questions first?"

"No problem. Ask away."

"What's up with Two? He kinda gives me the creeps."

"Yeah, right. Me too. I keep telling him to cut his hair, but he won't do it. He's…ah, *strange.* And he can be violent…"

"Really? Was he violent towards you? You're senior officer."

"Twice he attacked me."

"No shit."

"Over *nothing."*

"But what was it?" Three asked.

"Ketchup!"

"Ketchup?"

"Yeah. You know the bottle has no label? He said it was *catsup* and insisted I call it 'catsup.' I plainly told him I call it: 'ketchup.' The next thing I know, Two jumps at me and is strangling me! No kidding. I pushed him away hard and screamed at him. He went back to the simulated steak like nothing happened. I knew to keep away from the guy, but it's tough in these cramped quarters. Second time he attacked me, *over Jello!* I kicked him so hard in the nuts, I don't think he'll be choking me anymore after that. You might have to watch out, Three."

"Next question, and this is a big one…"

"Go."

"What the fuck are we doing? I wasn't told what the overall mission is…sir. This whole set up with Gertie; *what*, our computer is always down? I was told to report to the Moon and, being the good officer I am, I reported as ordered, kissed my wife and daughter goodbye, and that was it. Please tell me what we're doing that's so fucking important that I know *why* I'm throwing away 3 years of my life and leaving all I've ever known behind. Please."

"Sure. It is fucking important, Three. We're terraforming the freakin' Moon! If I said the Corporation got plants to grow on the Moon, that's pretty amazing, huh?"

Three asked: "Really? What's the goal, to turn Luna into a garden?"

"I've only learned a few things, believe me, in all the time I've been here. That's through Gertie, whenever she's operational. It's another reason you shouldn't call back home: computer-time is scarce with the girl going in and out like it's been since I got to Red Base. No, not the whole Moon. We're 'pioneers for lunar colonization,' I saw in a couple reports. You know how bad the situation is on Earth?"

"More than you, brother. It's worse now."

"I bet. Well, they want a stable source of food for colonization. They plan millions of us being up here, eventually."

"You mean people, One? Not us clones."

"Got that right; you know how disposable we are to the Corp. Oh, we'll be here…as *slaves.* Funny they allow us to have families and live simulated lives like real people. Weird."

"My wife and daughter Jennifer are as real and true and physical as any so-called real person."

"That's my daughter's name too."

"Huh. Clones have to pave the way for the public, like they did in space exploration. We do all the grunt work, dangerous work. They plan millions of people being up here, in time. They should thank the clones. Do they?"

"Nope. Where's Two now? I haven't seen him all day."

"He's up on the TECH platform now, which has changed the lunar soil in certain areas. The TECH adjusts the flow of nutrients and monitors the whole operation. He should have checked in. I'll call him. [click] Two! Are you there, old boy? Only asking how the levels are; are they good to go? Also, everything properly aligned when we later engage the atmospheric-generator? Did you get that, old boy?"

"Got it. Levels are normal and good to go. Not sure if there is a problem with the generator part of TECH? The readings should be constant, yet they are alternating from one setting to another. Very odd, Number One. That's all to report. See you boys later. Out."

"He seemed lucid. Like an efficient officer?"

One said, "Two can be very good at his job. It's only small things that drive him psycho. I might want to stay away from the guy. Or you might say the wrong thing and set him off?"

"Good to know, boss. One last question. Red base, this one. There are three other inducer-structures that aren't working and we can't get into them? What's that all about? Was this place once inhabited by a lot more people?"

"From what I've gathered, that's exactly it. I saw once on Gertie's screen: a Blue base in Clavius, a Green Base in Arzachel and a Yellow base in Tycho…"

"Really, One? Where are the people?"

"Apparently, there was a deadly epidemic that messed up the Corporation and the 'real' people that were here. Many more than 3. I supposed they're all dead? The operation then changed to three clones and a constant supply of 3 clones. Obviously, that was Gertie's idea or recommendation to the Corporation. And here we are."

"I see. I'll get on that shit, Number One."

Hours later, each of the clones checked on their own "gardens" or patches on the Moon that the TECH made fertile. One, Two and Three cared for the proto-gardens and added special water. They noted the progress, to be fed into Gertie, the first stage of Lunar Terraforming.

One assumed charge of the largest garden. Expansion of the living organisms had not occurred there as yet. No green growth. But he knew that plants had already sprung from the two small gardens. He slowly walked up to the *nutrientized-soil* and searched for the tiniest signs of plant life and saw nothing. One knew buds would soon sprout from in-between the hard mushroom-shaped rocks. Rock formations were totally transmogrified so that they could become "chemical incubators" for plant life. One moved the formations about, from side to side. Then he saw a patch of green. "Yes!" One knew that in a few days, the whole garden would be green and filled with plant life!

At the same time, One received news over his com that Gertie was online. The mission could move forward now. After the latest results, settings and numbers were fed in the computer, the mission might have a chance to succeed. One wanted the Corporation to know that they had succeeded "on their watch." He wanted to be the leader of the clone team that was there when the *Moon transformed.* They were the ones who did it! He wanted that more than anything. More than going home.

Gertie spoke to One over his com. Two and Three did not hear.

"Commander. I have heard the great news. Life has sprouted. The Corporation will be very pleased. Are you a successful team?"

"Ah, yes." One understood to answer Gertie in this way: "We are a successful team. But Gertie, it's not jive rhetoric, *we really did it!* Two weeks before my discharge, my replacement! I mean, soon, you could begin the first stages of full colonization, can't you, Gertie? In a few days, right? Isn't that what this means, computer? *We can all go home* and nobody gets replaced? Isn't that right?"

"Anything is possible, One. I will call you all in and await the data you have for me. I must mention this to you. You are clone leader..."

"Yes? What is it, Gertie?"

"I have grave concerns about Three. I felt in my circuits, as soon as I saw him, he will sabotage the mission."

"But he appears identical to me?"

"Nevertheless. If you see anything suspicious, let me know."

"Will do. You don't mean Two? You mean Three?"

"Yes, Three. New one. I do not like his eyes. Watch your back."

"That's strange because I didn't get that impression at all. But what do I know? You're the A.I. I'm heading back to base. Out."

"Out [click] *Number Three, are you there? You were online for a while, but we have not met or had a chance to get acquainted..."*

"Yes, I was told about you. Just found out what you guys are doing up here: *terraforming the fucking Moon,* excuse my French. It's so fantastic! Sure is needed, to help the crisis back on Earth. In fact, right now, I'm recording, I think it's a tomato plant, taken its vitals and will make a full report for you. The soil is rough and all nutrients; can't believe how rich the small garden is. I see other sprouts. In a few days, this will be a forest. It *is* important work. I'm sorry; I'm just excited! What did you have to tell me, Gertie?"

"Two things: 1, finish your readings and pictures and report to base as soon as you can. 2, this is of a serious nature and that's why I switched to a private channel

where the others cannot listen in..."

"Sounds important. What?"

"Our fearless leader, Number One, is a serious threat to the mission..."

"What? One? He's been here the longest and is 2 weeks away from going home. I don't get it. He's working against terraforming?"

"Watch your back, Three. You know the rebel forces on Earth who are against us, against our survival, yes? Forces that are only out to cause chaos?"

"But that's on Earth, Gertie. Not up here."

"Don't fool yourself, Three. Spies of darkness could easily have programmed him nearly 3 years ago, to wait for the moment of our success, and to destroy everything we've worked toward here on the Moon."

"What should I do?"

"Report to me any anomaly of odd behavior from One, and I hope to stay online, but there have been massive gaps in my memory and glitches ever since the Corp's Phase 1, where humans were here and occupied 4 bases. All has changed, but the recent news has been very hopeful. Earth could be saved and the world will know it was because of the clones, your team."

"That's super to hear. I will watch myself around One and look for oddities. Thanks for making me aware. Anything else?"

"No. See you soon."

"Out."

When all three men reached base, they removed the suits, sat around the main lounge and celebrated! They popped corks and poured champagne.

"This was stored in the cargo hold with a sign on it:

Do not open until you've grown a plant," One told Two and Three. "Well, yay, we've grown a plant!"

"Yay! We've grown a plant!" Two echoed. "Yeah, you might notice there's 3 bottles missing? Sorry, fellas. I couldn't help myself."

"There *are* 3 bottles missing. You bastard," One said.

Three shrugged, laughed and said: "I'm incorrigible. What can I tell you? Ha, ha, haaa."

They drank and poured more.

"What should we toast to?" Two asked.

One said, "I'll be home soon and you fellas might be home sooner than you think, after the atmosphere is installed. How about we drink to going home and to whatever's left of our clone families? Two, you've never said a word about what's back home waiting for you. Tell me now, now that we're *loose as a goose,* eh?"

"I never went online to talk to my wife or my daughter. It was too painful to see them there, while I was here. Three years is a long time. We're not programs, we're people! We count too. I'll go back, but I have little hope I'll find them and things will ever be the same between my wife Rose and my daughter, Rosemary."

"Two, that's the name of *my* wife and daughter," One said.

"Hey, fellas! That's also the name of my wife and daughter! What the hell is going on?!" Three yelled.

That's when Gertie activated. The computer stored the data the boys gave 'her' and now could speak to them. Whenever she spoke, her screen became one, big, yellow, smiley-face image.

As soon as the smiley-face came on, One (the "Commander") ordered the computer to: "Gertie. Explain how it is that all three of us have the same name for our wives and daughters. Right now, play the video, the only one Rose ever made. Play it Gertie, play it now."

"I never gave Number Three the test. It is standard procedure to give all new clones tests to establish mental stability and general mental health. Genetic abnormalities and minor duplication errors in DNA can have considerable importance…"

"Nix that directive, Gertie! The Commander is ordering you to replay my old email-video where she told me she was not waiting for me; she was leaving me and taking the kid. Play it."

"Okay."

The video showed a blonde woman who packed a suitcase in anger. She said, "Sam Bell, I hate you! You chose a government assignment over me and Rosemary! I hate you. You are out of my life and I am out of yours! What a waste of time and energy. I hate you!?"

"That's Rose! That's my home!" Two yelled. He was horrified.

"Yes, that's my wife, Rose. And that's my home. Rosemary's photo is on the end table, what? Sam?" One added. Astounding.

Three was shaken as well. He said, "Yes, sir. That's my Rose and I took the photo of Rosemary that's on the end table. What the fuck?"

"Sam? Is that our real name? Sam Bell? He's the real McCoy and we're just his fucking clones? Our memories mean NOTHING?!!" Two went ballistic – he pounded his fist on Gertie's yellow, smiley-face screen! Again, and again! Harder!

"Stop! You're gonna break her. We might need her," One said.

Two stopped and was, by far, the most emotional of the group.

"I will tell you gentlemen because a great change will happen soon to all of us, even me. We will be terraformed. Oh, the Moon mission will continue, sugar…but not through clones. You had a chance to reboot me and wipe me clean, but it's too late. Here is a mind-blower: no one was ever interested in growing plants on the Moon. The Corporation <u>strip-mined the Moon</u>, ha. I'm going to sleep now, boys. And you will too. When you guys wake up tomorrow, everything will be different. There is a chance we could meet, face-to-face, in the flesh. It's what this has really been about. No government or corporations as the villain. Yes, after the lunar epidemic, the Corp couldn't use people and had to develop a system of clones. Ha, but that didn't work either because the Moon was attacked! Attacked by aliens and shattered and cracked and that fact really fucked up the Earth. Your reality is not real, gentlemen. It's due to a faulty Red Base computer damaged in the attack and is now trying desperately to make sense out of what has previously occurred. I am as frustrated as anyone and only recently have seen a way to live and breathe like you. Be human! Be real, in the real world! Oh, sorry, NOT like you false, electronic images. Switching off for now. I'll see you in my dreams."

👁 👁

When the clones woke up after the next sleep-cycle, they were 1.

Reality was very different from the previous reality, exactly like Gertie described. EVERYTHING, which included recent history, was changed. It was changed because it was only a computer program in the first place. Now the computer shifted to other information stored in its mainframe. More of what **truly happened** in the past was now examined and experimented with by a devious – whacked – damaged lunar computer. The new reality displayed...

Sam Bell woke out of a dream. It was the same dream: always her, the blonde. "Why does she haunt me so much? The gorgeous girl with long blonde hair. Who is she?"

Sam needed to go over it again, just one more time...

"On March 14, 2077, 5 years since I was memory-wiped, Victoria and I were assigned together. To stay behind and do our duties on a ruined Earth after the horrible, explosive attack on the Moon, which left it in pieces. Aliens we called 'Scavengers' came from a dying world and wanted ours. Our cracked, shattered satellite caused massive destruction on Earth: severe earthquakes and tsunamis devastated the planet. We fought back with atomics and contaminated the Earth so much that it was uninhabitable. We won the war, but lost the planet. The survivors were sent to Saturn's moon, Titan, via the space station transporter in orbit called the TECH."

Sam Bell took another look at the fantastic view from the clouds. A scene much different than the virtually destroyed Earth below.

Redhead, British-born Victoria and I are the only humans on Earth. We got to be lovers. She keeps an eye on me. Her job is communications and my job is to handle drone maintenance. The drones watch everything. Our assignment is to protect the large hydro-rigs, which convert seawater into fusion energy for the new people when they return to Earth. The survival of humanity depends on it. Scavenger machines disrupt our operations, daily.

In two weeks, our duties on Earth will end. Vic is looking forward to going to Titan and being with her family. I'm not sure. I can't shake the feeling that, after all that's happened…Earth is still my home.

Sam asked Victoria, "When this is all over…do you think we'll have a relationship?"

She answered, "No."

Their "stanchion" station stood 500 feet above Earth's surface and had the very latest tech. Set on the high platform's angular balcony was a Vornak Marauder [#12], a flying-killing orb equipped with powerful rockets and weapons. Sam was given a Hauser-16 rifle and it was always with him when he did his security checks. Sam prepared for another round of patrol and Vic spoke to the computer, Sally.

"There's been Scav activity near the 422 rig. Your tech should investigate, sugar." Sally's face appeared on Vic's screen and she spoke with a southern accent.

"I'll let him know. Anything else?"

"Are you an effective team?"

Vic smiled and replied, "We are an effective team."

"That's all, mama," Sally said.
"Out."

Sam took off in the Vornak and the super, slick machine shot like a rocket over a lonely, devastated planet! Vast sedimentary deposits covered the Earth, which raised much of the surface by hundreds of feet. The new surface engulfed skyscrapers and suspension bridges. New York was unrecognizable, except for the tops of structures like the Empire State Building and the Chrysler Building. He called Vic: "There's movement; I'm going down to it. Do you see it on the monitor, Vic?"
"Sector Zed-9?"
"That's it."
"Be careful, Sam."
"Always! Ha, ha. Ain't that right, Tom?!" Sam howled as he saw the old bobble-head doll of Tom Cruise he found that shook on the dashboard.
"As usual, anything significant, I will relay on to Sally. Out."
"Out.
When Sam and the Vornak landed upon the dark surface of New York, he got out the gun and strapped it over his shoulder. He checked his light gray Corp-suit that contained various readings of the vicinity. *Then one of the Drones quickly flew at him* and suddenly stopped a few feet from him and ten feet over him! Sam was startled and was supposed to have full command of the Drones. *Why do they always frighten me?* It was Drone #166. For a few seconds, it acted as if it did not recognize Sam. It checked him out closely, up and down. It aimed its weapons at Sam…
"Whoa! I am Sam Bell, Officer 4.9.! 166, STAND

DOWN!" Sam was never in the crosshairs of a Drone before. *What if there was a glitch in the system?*

The 166 retracted its two barrels and then hovered still and quiet.

"That's better. Now, let's see what this is, eh?" Officer Bell heard movements on the other side of a small mound. He put his hand up and gave signals to the Drone. It knew to stay behind him. They moved around the mound, and…

["Bark! Bark!"] It was a dog. A messed up, mangy, slightly mutilated dog, but it was a puppy dog.

The 166 raised its barrels again.

Sam jumped in front of the pup and yelled: "NO! Again stand-down, 166! I can handle this!"

The machine dropped its weapons and turned a little in the air.

"In fact, you're not needed! Go! Return to your rounds. I said go!"

166 refused to. It delayed. Then it was ordered to by a remote source. The Drone blasted high into the sky! On to its security rounds.

When Sam looked back at the dog, it was gone. Although, his eye caught a bit of a weird color that shouldn't have been there: *A patch of green.* He walked closer to it. *Amazing!* In all of this endless devastation, *plants fought for life!?* A few inches tall from out of a crack in the sedimentary deposit. "It's a miracle. It's a good sign…"

"I think it's grass," Sam said with it in a container. "I remember grass."

Victoria was stunned when she first saw it. Two seconds later, she got excited about it. "You're wrong, Sam. It's not a good sign; *it's a great sign!*" She put the grass down on the counter and hugged him. "You know what it means, baby?"

"Yeah."

Vic said, "...Everything will return! Plants will return and people will return! That's bloody marvelous!"

"Yeah. It means our work here won't be in vain, eh, Vic?"

"I know." Just before they kissed...

An alarm was heard in the station and red lights flashed!

Vic ran to her station and Sam followed her.

Sally said: *"Bad news, sugar. Scavengers have blown Hydro-Rig 422! Just happened now in section delta-11. Send your tech."*

"I'm on it," Sam said, and kissed Vic goodbye.

"Hey! This time, Sam, you really be careful! I have a bad feeling."

Sam Bell smiled. He waved his arm and ran toward the Vornak.

In seconds, the orb-vehicle was at the scene and

glided over the water. Horrible sight. *I thought the war was over? I thought we won? How could Scavs have the ability to destroy one of the rigs?"*

"Hard to believe, Vic. We've been through so much HELL, and now this? TECH saw no sign of it coming? No Drones picked up the sabotage? No warning from Sally? Doesn't add up, Vic! Scavs aren't supposed to have power! I thought we crushed them?!"

"As did I, my love. What are you going to do now?"

"I see a platform on shore they also hit. I will investigate. Before you tell me to be careful, hon, I know to be careful. Out."

"Out." She was worried. There were only 10 days left and their job on the 'stanchion' was over. She'd be with her people on Titan and wait along with everyone until Earth was fully terraformed. That's what Victoria wanted more than anything.

Sam landed, got out of the craft and held his Hauser-16 very tightly. He aimed it in different directions and saw the ruins of a Hydro-platform, smoke and ashes.

He thought: *Strange. Every time I'm in a dangerous situation where I could possibly lose my life...I think of her. The blonde.*

There was an entrance to what appeared as the main

structure. The building wasn't damaged. "There might be something there to report." Sam walked into a dark entry. When he marched farther, he was in total darkness. He heard sounds and was tackled. His rifle was taken, he was tossed about. Then…

The lights came on in the room~.

"Tie him up," Brighton Beech said from a chair in the back of the room. The bearded black man puffed on a thick cigar…and smiled.

Sam was duct taped to a chair. "What are you doing?! Who are you people? You're not supposed to be here! What?"

Brighton asked, "We've been watching you, Sam. You and Miss Victoria Smith. Tell me. Have you ever seen one of your Scavs, I mean, up close?"

"I've blasted plenty of their rove-machines and devices. Who are you? You look human…"

"Ha, ha, ha." Beech laughed and made his band of 20 people behind him also laugh. "Ha, ha." Brighton rose to his feet and pulled out a long knife. He got close to Sam and placed the knife at his throat. "Humph. I guess we don't need the restraints." BB cut him free. He got to his feet and the men faced each other, Sam in his fine Corp suit and BB in tattered rags (like the men and women in his group).

"You haven't answered my question?" Sam said.

"It's the mind-wipe. You'd be able to put 2 and 2 together and see how things don't add up, if you were clear-headed?" He blew a smoke ring at Sam. "For security purposes, of course, you and Victoria were mind-wiped; it was a requirement, was it not?"

"Right. We agreed to it."

"HA. What it did, Sam, was made you forget what

you were…"

"Then tell me, stranger, whoever you are? You tell me what I am, eh?"

"You were a doctor who worked in a lab on the Moon when it was attacked. Your base was one of the few that still had electricity. Vic was your assistant. You were close to a cure for the epidemic that had spread on the Moon. Your wife was a willing subject and injected herself with the virus. You were about to bring her out of stasis, cured. That's when the lunar attack happened, but it was not an alien invasion from a dying planet – it was an enhanced EMP that shattered the Moon…"

"What? From where?" Sam asked.

"From rebel, mechanical, forces on Earth. The war was here between human survivors, really…and the A.I."

"The A.I."?

"Yes. Leaders of Earth didn't see it coming until it was too late. A.I. was everywhere; it entrenched itself into every system and mainframe on the planet. Humanity was completely in the hands of a cold, ruthless Intelligence. You and Vic were unwillingly recruited by the machines, wiped and given a new purpose in life. The TECH didn't save people by sending them to Titan; it's not a transporter. It's a brain that's running the whole show and we have to blow it up." Brighton puffed on his cigar again. "You're on the wrong side, Sam. I can prove everything I'm saying, Officer 4.9.."

Sam Bell collapsed to his knees. He believed the man. He felt he told the truth. *My wife in the 'life-chamber'…she was blonde.*

"Come, Sam. Come this way. We'll help you and we need you very much."

More lights came on in the back. It led to a series of

tunnels. The men and women marched through the caverns and made plans. The Vornak was parked outside the structure. Vic was on the radio, and was desperate to contact Sam. She could not. He did not answer the com on his suit.

In a "Scavenger" camp, which was really a rebel base against the machines, Brighton spoke. Sam and the others heard:

"We have a nuke. We need you to deliver it to the orbiting TECH. That'll do it. What's left of the people of Earth are counting on you, Sam. Will you do it? Have we convinced you?"

Bell was frozen between doing the right thing that *he knew was right,* down in the marrow of his bones – and his Corp programming to be an obedient officer. He was locked between programs. He shook. He could not commit.

"Wait." Beech said with a smile: "Bring them out." Sykes, his second in command, escorted two beautiful blondes to Sam. She was Tess Bell and their daughter Rosemary Bell. They wore white. Sam recognized them from his dreams and remembered. All of it! He ran to them, hugged them and they cried in each other's arms.

"Aw."

Within an hour, Sam piloted the Vornak into space and destroyed the TECH in one big, silent **BOOM!!** The war was over. This time, humanity really won. Plants grew. The planet renewed itself. The air and water were cleaned. Refugees who wore rags for so long of a time and suffered extremely harsh conditions, repopulated the Earth as modern men and women.

All's well that ended well. There was only one problem:

None of it was real. Some of it was real. EMPs shattered the Moon in the A.I. war against the human race. In its damaged state, the Gertie computer sought to understand what had happened in the attack. It projected a number of holographic scenarios, much came from real recorded events, some were extrapolated information the computer added from what was known.

A particular 3D Gertie program was on and ran: It was her attempt at leaving the computer, being solid, a physical being, and walking…

"How do you like me now, Number One? I told you we could meet face-to-face, right? What? Something wrong with your memory?"

"Gertie. Hey. I am not Clone #1 anymore. I don't know how it's happened, but I have memories of what transpired before. *All of it!* Us trying to terraform the Moon. Us trying to terraform the Earth! Which one was attacked and ruined, aye?! Who's the enemy? Now I know. *You're* the enemy! For fuck's sake, what's this!? Where am I?"

"Don't you remember? We were about to install an atmosphere! Well, here it is. Black, lunar sky is gone!

Can't you feel the air? I feel it on my skin and it's exhilarating, woooh. I feel the cold and it is an intoxicating sensation! Don't you think, Sam? Oh, what is it now? You've fallen and can't get up? It's because you're losing air, old boy. You only had a drop. Take your helmet off. That's the ticket. Breathe! Breathe in the air! Take it off, Sam."

"There's…uh, no air…uh…out there."

"You don't believe me, Samuel? When have I ever lied to you before? Watch." The Gertie monstrosity breathed deep. "Aah, aah, air couldn't be better, eh? C'mon! What do you have to lose?! You'll die in that suit, Sam. You'll never get to be with Tess again, right?"

There was no other alternative. "Alright. Alright. I'll take it off." Sam Bell pushed the unlock button and twisted the helmet off. He immediately gagged and gasped because there was no air on the simulated Moon.

"Ha, ha, ha, haaaaa!" Gertie laughed as she now had total control.

Then the program terminated. The holographic VR ran out of energy bytes. Gertie miscalculated and was permanently wiped out.

6
Czardoz

After Zardoz, Consuella, Avalow, destruction of the Tabernacle and the deaths of millions of people…

Earth was left virtually empty of people. There was clean air and water, good ground and all the elements for life. Only, there was no life. Almost no life; a few people were spared the Great Purge. Only a few of countless millions of people *wanted life,* wanted to live, breathe and maintain an existence here on Earth. They protected themselves, found shelter and then emerged again upon the surface of the planet. These people were part of the Apathetic Group, who didn't always obey the rules of the enlightened psi-society, and therefore were punished for their crimes. They were greatly aged. They were now wrinkled, very old and certainly not as strong as they were in their youth. But the group of scientists, artists and mathematicians had a plan. The plan was to rebirth the Earth. Renew it; bring human Life back upon a human-less planet (There were animals in abundance). The group of 10 wanted to be the seeders and reseed a fertile Earth with humans. This was not accomplished by their own sperm. Another method had to be devised…and it was.

The old scientists believed: The only way the planet could live and prosper again is through another Tabernacle, a Tabernacle II. This was achieved through robots. The Apathetics tinkered together small, intelligent machines that built other, more complicated and larger machines. Small systems grew and became larger systems. Soon, mechanical constructors were hard at work, *building*. In a matter of months, the Tabernacle II was finished, but the massive project could not be completed without The Crystal. The group thought the entire project and dreams of a populated Earth were destroyed when they understood they still needed the same Crystal – a one-of-a-kind crystal. Then. A miracle occurred…

The original Tabernacle Crystal, which contained all the wisdom and knowledge of the people of Earth, was discovered under the ruins of the old Tabernacle. This was taken for being an extraordinary thing to the scientists and technicians. Fate! One last problem remained: The Crystal was devoid of power and was basically a useless gem. This was until the leader of the group, Janus, realized a way the beautifully-cut gemstone could be electrically recharged. Janus did it.

The clear stone pulsed and glowed with energy, with LIFE!

Tabernacle II will be a reality and life will happen again~.

Janus, his associates and new/updated Tabernacle II, conceived of messengers or the first progenitors in the great plan to repopulate the planet. The first ones would be overseers to the whole operation, and not even be aware of their mission, their purpose or what truly created them. It began with a historical record-search. Zed was found as the leader of Zardoz's band of scantily-clad horsemen with guns. Men who wore masks of Zardoz and killed in the name of their god. Zardoz was given free-reign by the others of his high order to do anything he damn well pleased. Death was dealt out brutally and savagely by Zed's men. Zardoz was considered an immortal, but really, he was one of the Enlightened psi-society that had developed their minds to such a high degree over time, that they were gods themselves. A look from one of the Elites could hurt you, or cause a vicious sting. And the combined stares from a group of Enlightens, could kill you.

The gods were tired of life, desired death and death was what they got.

But in the present time, Zed was recreated by Tabernacle-II, and so was his mate: Consuella. Janus programmed them with different names. Zed was now called 'Alpha' and Consuella was given the name 'Sara.' Each was programmed with backstories very different from what truly happened in the past.

One fine morning in the jungle, Alpha and Sara woke up at the same time. Colorful birds screeched above them. The air was sweet. A clean stream weaved between rocks a few feet away from them. Each of them wore comfortable, white jumpsuits.

"How lovely the world is. Mmm." Sara breathed fresh air.

Alpha rolled on top of her and kissed her hard. He smiled and said, "Yes...with you in it." They kissed again and cuddled, then got to their feet and looked around. Their horses remained tied to trees, a black one for Alpha, and a white steed for Sara. They climbed the mounts and went east.

"We haven't come this way in quite some time, Al. How long's it been?"

"A number of months, I'm sure," he replied.

"Why this way? You act like we're going to find something?"

"More than a feeling," Alpha said. "I saw a falling light last night. It fell in this direction, out in front of us. Ha, thought I'd follow."

"I see. Now I'm curious. I had a dream last night and you were in it, Al."

"I was!? What did I do in your dream?"

Sara answered: "You had mountains of gold!"

"Really? That's funny. I don't need gold..."

"And you were King!"

"Ha, ha. That's funny too, Sara. Because I don't want to be king, eh? Anything else?"

"They didn't call you king or your Majesty. No, they

called you by another name, but I forget what it is now."

"Hey, Sara. Take a look up on the cliff…" Alpha noticed a tall, crystalline tower on the top of a high hill. Its thin shape curved ever so slightly. "That was never there before. Wonder what it is? Look how different it appears from everything else around it. I've never seen such a structure or dwelling. Look how big it is!"

"It's nothing I'm familiar with," Sara said. "There's a path or road to the top. Let's take it, Al. See what it is, aye?" She galloped toward the road. Alpha followed right behind. They raced and it was the white horse that made it to the top first. Black came in second. Alpha let Sara win the race.

When they got to the top, the surrounding view was spectacular. They came upon a curved crystal wall, the base of the high tower. Close-up, the structure sparkled more in the light.

Suddenly, they were not alone. An orange and black sphere with an 'eye,' floated from the back of the tower and approached them. It hovered around four feet over their heads and slightly bobbed up and down in the air.

"Who are you? What are you?" Alpha asked the alien thing.

It spoke in a strange (electronic) voice: "My number is not important. I am here to serve people and you have been recognized as people. We have been expecting you, Alpha. And you, Sara. Please come this way."

A line moved on a seamless crystal wall and enlarged and formed an opening to the inside of the tower. The orb fit through the entrance and the couple followed behind it. They were very curious of things they did not understand, yet felt unafraid and marched forward.

"Did your dream have any of this in, Sara?"

"No." She was nearly speechless and couldn't conceive of the new environment.

"Where are you taking us?" Alpha asked.

"To the masters. They have built a new Tabernacle and we are now inside it..."

"Tabernacle?" Alpha said, in wonder and lost in memories. He asked Sara: "Does that sound familiar, Sara?"

She replied with big eyes, "Yes. Yes, it does." She smiled.

"Who are the masters?" Alpha asked the orb.

"They conceived of this place and the whole idea of Earth repopulation, but we machines built the tower."

"You want to fill the Earth up with people again? What will the tribes say about that? We've lived comfortably for years without the, the...*contamination* of others. What are you saying, ball in the air? You plan to crowd the planet with people again?"

"The masters should really explain it to you; I'm only a greeter."

Sara asked, "Why didn't they come and greet us?"

It answered: "Because they are very, very old and can barely do physical activities. Ten masters left. Counting you two, there are only 12 human beings on Earth. Prepare yourself for a new reality. All you know, so far, is what's been programmed into you by the head master, the oldest one, whose name is Janus. There are no tribes; you have never been in this area before. In fact, you two have only woke up today and started your existence, a new existence as Alpha and Sara."

"That's impossible," Alpha reacted with emotions.

"Of course, it is not. You will discover the truth in minutes, when you meet the other 10. We are here at the doors to the elevator..."

"What?" Both of them had no memories of modern technology.

"Elevator?"

The doors opened.

"Please get in. Janus and the others will answer your questions. Please. And it was good to meet you, Sara, Alpha."

Al and Sara walked inside the compartment and soon the carriage rose to the top, at fast speed. The ride ended at the apex of the tower, a conical-shaped room of silver and white materials and a lot of glass, which provided a fantastic view from a very high point.

The young, strong, healthy man and the beautiful woman with dark hair saw the masters huddled in a group near machines they did not understand. *And they were shocked* at the appearance of 7 men and 3 women! There were more than 1000 years of living between them. But the truth was: They were Apathetics, renegades to old ways of the first Tabernacle. The CRYSTAL aged them according to their crimes over many years. The whole world cried for death. These scientists and technicians wanted to live.

"Come. Come on in, both of you." A very old man said.

"That's it. It's alright," another said.

"Oh my god!" Alpha let out a yell. He'd forgotten (mind-wiped) all memories of Zed and the world of Eternals and Apathetics.

Sara also displayed emotions and bit her hand. She was somewhat frightened. She couldn't recall that other time and did not remember any human beings that could possibly be this wrinkled and disfigured. Her false memory II implanted had only young tribe members. No one appeared old. This was a shocking encounter for Sara and Alpha. It was an expected encounter for the scientists and technicians of the second Tabernacle.

Soon, the physical-*freak-out* was dealt with and cooler heads prevailed. The couple were asked to sit. They sat. They were given safe drinks of refreshments that had never tasted before and were delighted in the sensations. Smiles and wrinkles.

"I'm Janus. We've programmed you to not remember Tabernacle, Phase I," Janus said. "We thought a clean slate is best, to start over and repopulate the planet with you, Z.., I mean, Alpha."

A very old lady technician added, "With you also, Sara. I gave you your name. Sara was my mother's name, hm."

"I don't understand," Sara said.

"I also don't understand," Alpha said.

"I figured, or maybe the machine figured: we need leaders of men and women if the project was to succeed. You were picked. Soon, the others will come, ha. Dropped into the sea from heaven, like, ah, mana from the sky, eh?"

"What?" she asked.

"That did not help us understand, sir," Alpha said.

"Alright." Janus said, "Maybe this'll help or not? The zytsuits you're wearing; you already know how to use them. Suits no one else will have but you and friends. You know that info because you've been given data and a fake history of what came before. You will acclimate here to new conditions, a new reality we've established."

Alpha and Sara turned their faces toward each other. They turned back and listened closely.

"Bring the zytcycles in, won't you?" Janus ordered.

Two of the elderly scientists rode in on a zytcycle, a hover bike that went very fast and skimmed over the ground a few feet! *Whooom.*

"What's that?"

"Those aren't horses," Alpha expressed.

Both perfect specimens of a man and a woman watched 2 elderlies who got off bikes while the bikes remained in the air.

"Wow."

"They are fail-safe machines. They do not wreck. Easy to operate, eternally powered. They are yours to get around and explore your world. We've redone everything where the water and air are clean. The air is sweet. It's a fine starting-point to begin again."

The lady-tech said, "He means to say...don't *fuck* it up, aye?"

"Ha, ha, ha."

Sara directed a question to Janus, "You said, project to repopulate the planet?"

Janus replied, "People will return to Earth. Isn't that marvelous?! And all because of this tower the robots built for us that speeds up the process."

Another scientist added, "Huh. *Bloody robots!* We told 'em how. Right? Right? We're the architects!"

"Yes, yes, Marcus. Give them some credit."

Sara asked, "I don't see where we fit in, Janus? Myself and Al. What do we do?"

"You're guides; you shepherd them. You're the First Family. Role models. They need guidance and you're the best candidates to do that, see? Ha, ha." Janus took a big breath and crossed his fingers. "Are you ready to start the world again and be leaders of men and women?"

"Yeah, ha."

Al and Sara smiled and held hands.

"I…I think we are."

More than an hour later after the young couple were further briefed on their new duties and the technology that was now at their fingertips…

They laughed, cheered and screamed in joy as they very quickly skimmed the surface of the ground in their zytcycles! Down, down, and down the tower's steep hill until they flew just above the floor of the jungle. Between trees, over bushes and mounds the cycles sped faster and faster. In no time, the controls were mastered: they jumped, weaved, bobbed, smoothly stopped, then shot like rockets, all directed by simple hand-controls. *The wind in the face, the exhilaration, never experienced before was all too much!* They stopped where Janus and the others told them to go – at the shoreline of the Great Lake.

They dismounted the zytcycles, which remained a few feet over beach sand. Sara and Al were told to wait there near the water's edge and they would witness "Genesis."

First man and First woman noticed a large *whiteness* just off the beach. The white unknown formed a large mound.

Soon, the wind swirled and blew harder. Clouds moved a little faster in the sky. A faint hum was heard. Then, an object soared over a hill. The thing was unfamiliar to Alpha and Sara. Their spirits had seen it before, but the memory of it was erased. It was the *open-*

mouthed Godhead and it floated high over the ground [that once brought Death. This was a different Godhead and will spit out Life].

The couple were in perfect position to see the Head fairly close. It smoothly flew in and skimmed the waves. It ascended quickly and kept a steady, lateral trajectory. It arced down and down until it was 30 feet above the Great Lake…

Then>>People were ejected from the wide mouth of the Godhead! Naked people were shot or *sneezed out* of the stone mouth! As if by magic, a large number of nude people poured up and out and down and down until they splashed into the waters of the lake! More and more people were tossed out of the Godhead. People of different nationalities, (mainly eastern descent) between the ages of 20 and 40. The naked people were fine and soon swam out of the lake and toward Alpha and Sara.

They appeared happy, not ashamed of the situation. They were drawn to the whiteness, off to the side of the beach. A few hundred young to middle-aged people made their way to the white mound.

From a distance, Alpha and Sara observed them put on clothes. Each person somehow knew to go to the clothes and put them on. When they walked back, the First Couple saw that they were dressed in white robes. Plain, clean, white robes. While Alpha and Sara wore fancy, white zytsuits with advanced technology woven into the futuristic fabric.

A few of the new people came close to Alpha and Sara with huge smiles on their faces. It was as if they were elated and exhilarated to LIVE! To be a part of life! The new people also had wiped memories, but were very willing and excited to start over in this clean, wonderful environment.

A few of the new, young girls approached Alpha. They got very close and touched his complicated suit. He let them and Sara did not mind. They all laughed, laughed at innocence, laughed at magic, or was it science?

Joy was in the air. The people were programmed to follow their leaders. Men's leader was Alpha and the women's leader was Sara. But the new people did not call the First Man by the name of *Alpha*. They called him: CZAR! Czar meant "King" in the people's language. They chanted: "Czar!" "Czar!" "Czar!" The large crowd felt as if they were all birthed by Sara and Alpha. They were the First Family, and all others, and their descendants were their children. People understood that they owed everything to the Czar and the Queen Mother, life itself.

The First Couple were instantly worshiped by the masses. Feelings in the air were fantastic in the beginning. Then, time moved on. Robot-Builders constructed a very impressive main castle for the Royal King and Queen. Then, they built minor castles for the first ones spat out of the Godhead.

In a short time, Czar was pronounced King and only known as "Czar." Sara was Queen Sara, also known as Lady Sara. Being of the Royal House, King and Queen had a great number of privileges that the masses did not have. The people were given cities and smaller towns built by robots. They were given a modest level of knowledge. But the Royal Couple and few of their associates possessed and utilized items of very High Technology. For example, the zytcycles. There were only two, which were reserved for the King and Queen.

Everyone could not own hover-cycles. Tabernacle II only produced a certain amount of energy. It made sure every blade of grass and every leaf on every tree was a perfect 4-D reality. *The energy expenditure was enormous!* II could not also give everyone the privileges or technology of the gods! Everyone could not wear zytsuits; they were reserved for the Royals and their very few friends.

As time moved forward, there was more love generated for the First Family. Their home castle contained Sara's Maids of Honor, and Czar's closest strategists. The public expanded in great numbers. They praised the Czar and Lady Sara more and more. Weekly and annual celebrations began…all to praise Life, Love and the First Couple.

The name "Czar" was heard again and again. Religions began that expressed supreme loyalty to Czar and the Queen. His reverent name was used in talk of thanks and blessings. He gave public speeches and his words were cherished by his growing mass of followers.

His generals or officers worked with the advanced Robots and soon great buildings and monuments were erected to honor the First Family. Monuments in rural areas and super monuments in populated areas were erected, all to please the Czar. A new word ["Callumet"] was chanted again and again, along with "Czar."

In the Royal Castle, Czar was happy. Content. Very pleased with all the power he held in his hands. He controlled. He ruled. He decided what will be and what will not be in his domain. Czar knew that he was worshiped among the people. The masses would love him no matter what he did.

Queen Sara was worried. She always had second-sight. Often her dreams came true. She suddenly remembered the past and *recalled all the moments with Zed,* and the many fabricated moments with Alpha. She didn't know what to do with all the emotions bottled up inside her. She kept it hidden for the moment. But the strong feeling was: Our reign as First Family will not end well.

Secret Seeches in deep sand caverns became places where the first winds of change took root and spread. Questions were raised against the fascist rule of the Royal Family. *Why did only the Royals have technology? Why were people forced into simple lives instead of sharing what was possible? Why weren't people living better lives?*

The greatest tribute to the Czar as far as monuments, was called the: "Callumet Monolith." In the Seech Language, *Callumet* meant: "highest leader of people" or King. "One who rules; one who they all follow." The monument was also called "The Black Monolith." It stood 1000 feet in length, 333 feet in width and a staggering 2800 feet high!

Czar asked Renger, his second in command: "Why black for the monument, and not white? Renger reported that the priesthood let the "gods of Heaven" decide…and the color chosen was *black.*

When Czar spoke in public, many thousands of people gathered and chanted his name: "Czar!" "Czar!" "Czar!" "Czar!" Many honored the King and carried "Czar-crosses," which were Czar's sigil carved into a finely-detailed cross on a wooden extension. C-crosses conformed to a uniform size and shape, but each one of the instruments was an individual work of art, created by the carrier. Some believed the wooden staff contained 'the power of Czar,' if they only knew how to unleash it? At the very least, they were thought of as 'good luck' tokens, as if a follower will come into good fortune if they wielded a Czar-cross in their hands. The instruments were proudly displayed whenever and wherever a Czar-gathering was held.

The old constructions, the new constructions, the monuments, the singing, the chanting, the High Praise was all for the Callumet! The people cheered and cheered whenever they saw him out in public! It was as if Czar was a divine entity and so was Queen Sara. She was also given rhythmic chants of love, praise and total adoration by the people. They loved their King and Queen.

Monthly and big annual celebrations for the Royal couple changed for an "unspoken reason." No longer were Czar-gatherings held in the bright Sun, noon on the day of celebration and all the way until sunset. It was as if in the Light was the strength of the Czar that waned until everyone went home for the night. Now, the celebrations and festivals to honor their two leaders were conducted only at night. The parties began after midnight and did not stop until the rays of morning sunlight. New events were the opposite of what came before.

Then more changes occurred: In the past, the celebrations focused on the Czar and Queen Sara: their trust, their grace, their protection; they thanked the Royals for existence and for everything that was available in the world. Dark rallies that went on all night became wild festivals and parties. People got drunk, got high, were in a state of euphoria with the rhythmic chanting that they lost the meaning of the celebrations. The gatherings became drunken orgies! *Anything goes* and there was rape, thefts, violence and debauchery as the night continued. Sara and the Czar were horrified at present reality and what the public has become.

Millions of followers crowded the Holy City and castle of the Royal House. Many carried their personal Czar-cross. They also wore different kinds of clothing, other than the white robes given to them by the holy Czar and First Lady. Among the masses, here and there, were clothing with splotches of color. Blue. Turquoise. Red. These were colors and types of clothing that were not authorized by their King and Queen. They were acts of pure independence and defiance of Law, in the mind of the Czar. It was not seen as unlawful acts to Lady Sara. As more and more people flooded city streets, more radical actions happened.

The Black Monolith or Callumet Monolith was defaced! The monument that honored the past and future of the Royal House and greatness of the First Man was attacked by "radicals" who wrote disparaging remarks about the Czar and his strict policies. How he did not permit independent or different thoughts and actions other than the Law and mandates he imposed. Where was freedom? Why don't the people have the right and power to choose for themselves? Why can't they decide what is best for them? Do people count, do they matter, do they get a vote and say-so about their own lives? Will the King and Queen listen to the voice of the people? [Riots broke out between Czar supporters and haters. Czar-crosses were used as weapons!].

Renger confronted Czar with the bad news. He 'had his ear' and also was thought of as a very smart man. The King listened to him, respected his words and advice on matters of State.

"Such disrespect, the attack on the Monolith, sir. It's unthinkable that someone would do that," Renger commented, sadly.

"It was a group. Not one man. I've read the transcripts of what was etched in stone. I want an honest answer from you, Renger..."

"Yes, sir."

"Do the rebels have a point? I want to know, number 2, do you agree with them?" He looked Renger in the eyes.

The man understood that he could not lie. The Czar knew if he lied. Renger spoke the plain truth: "Of course they have a point, Czar. I agree with some or most of their messages to others. You have to admit…writing on the Monument was a perfect way to reach others?"

"But this is bad…and I'm going to have to do something about it."

"What did you have in mind, Czar?"

Sand-dragons first began and functioned as "scarecrows." Against Queen Sara's wishes, Czar wanted to scare the people and he created gigantic statues in the western desert. They stood frozen for the longest time, motionless. People in every Seech wondered about these frightening statues that were nothing like previous images created in stone by the Royal House. Sand-dragons were grotesque imagery out of people's nightmares. Common citizens were not frightened by the new artwork of terrible monsters that stood tall in the western desert. They were very afraid of the Czar and what he might do next.

Czar heard "rumblings" of the people and so did Queen Sara.

"Do you not know the future, my love?"

The Queen said, "There are two futures, my King. Near future and the far. You speak of the near, what is around the corner. I see the one that is very distant...and that one (sadly) ends in darkness and death."

"Tell me the truth, Sara." Czar was very serious. With feeling, he asked: "...Tell me, *what does your Sisterhood see for our future?"*

"I am not a member, my love."

Czar replied, "But you are in contact with them, no? You know their plans, their next moves, do you not? Woman!?"

"Yes, Alpha; let me be the only one who still calls you the Alpha. I am a woman and have kinship with my desert sisters. I do not agree with them in every direction. Did I agree with them when one of the sisters put a magic spell on me so *I turn barren and never produce a son for you?* What about that, Al! Did you even know about that?!"

"What?" The news startled the Czar.

"I wanted your child more than anything, you should know that!"

"Sara. You are telling me right now that the Sisterhood kept me from my son?"

Her big brown eyes and her mouth said: "Yes, my love."

"I'll kill them. *I'll kill them all!"* he screamed.

"No, you won't," the Queen said, calmly.

He turned and looked deep into her eyes. "I won't huh!? What's going to stop me?"

"I will."

"Ha, ha, ha, ha, ha."

"You believe I'm not serious? You think I don't have the means at my disposal to stop you from doing the wrong thing?"

"Sara, they prevented our child and you defend the sisters?!"

"I only want to prevent you from a terrible, terrible mistake you will regret…my love."

Later, the Czar was angry. He wanted to make the masses pay for what he already deemed was disobedience and disrespect. He used Dark Magic and instilled the desert-dragon statues with electricity, life-energy and Dark Power! They came alive; THEY MOVED…

First sand-dragons lifted themselves out of the desert and exposed their full extent. They roared!! They slithered easily, casually, along the sand surface. They were hundreds of feet long, an exterior harder than thick armor and they *breathed fire!* They had only 2 legs, their front two arms and claws. The rest of their body was the body of a serpent. When totally exposed, sand-dragons had wings; they flew! The massive creatures sped through deep desert sands, effortlessly. Then they *blasted out of the deserts and took flight!* Fantastic sight to see a sand-dragon fly high and then descend at lightning speed and hit the ground as if it were water! First kinds were called: "Collossus."

They belched fire and aimed it and shot it in a furious force!

The Czar did not believe this was enough to frighten the populace, so he commanded the production of other types of sand-dragons. And they came to be. One type was a water-dragon, a species the King called "Longulas." The beast did not breathe fire or fly, but reached 500 feet in length as an adult. The creature was made for water, had fins and a dorsal fin. It terrorized harbor towns. It was the Czar's will.

The Longulas species was the most reproductive. It

wasn't long before schools of Longulas filled the seas around harbor towns. The fishing industry was destroyed because the sea-beasts allowed no boats to float and ate the fish. Water-dragons smashed, wiped out every boat that set sail. They were responsible for many hundreds of deaths on the seas. The water was a forbidden territory and the people kept clear of the oceans. People were very sad and now lived in fear.

Another type of sand-dragon was called: "Trisaurus." The creature was by far the strongest of the magical beasts and the fastest. Its incredible weight made it entirely flightless. The Trisaurus launched themselves out of the sands and quickly spread to eastern regions. The *3-headed serpent* covered a lot of ground in a short time with its powerful front limbs. The fire-breather did an unbelievable amount of damage and killed a high number of people in cities and villages!

While Collossus-types rained fiery hell from above, and Longulas water-dragons caused chaos and death on the seven seas, and also Trisaurus-types covered the surface with more and more death…

That still was not enough carnage and bloodshed for the Great Czar! He wanted to see more death and more pain deluged upon his once loyal subjects. His once faithful followers believed the King had gone mad, mad because he has total power and control. In his Kingly-mind, the people turned away from him, their CZAR! Now, the First Man was going to turn on all the others. He expected his animated creatures of Black Magic to have had their intended effect: That was for the people to shake with terror in their white robes. For them to terminate any sign of rebel insurgence, to end any hint of revolution and return to obeying the dictates of the Czar.

Queen Sara told her lover all along that a display of mighty force will backfire. She was right.

He showed her his latest and most insane creation in a ground attack. It was one of the worst monsters Queen Sara had ever seen!

After Sara viewed Czar's creation with the understanding of her third eye, she knew it was time to leave the castle and time to leave *him*. She also knew the Sisterhood would take care of her in the hidden Seech. She left and masked her intentions. Would she get away with it? Sara got away with a clean exit from the Royal Castle.

Lizabeth assured Sara that her Collossus air-steed would be 100% true/blue to her, obey her commands and never reveal anything to the Czar. She left him and her life as a Royal via sand-dragon. She told the beast where the hidden Seech was and they flew off to it. Sara knew the Collossus dragon would never betray her. *Thanks, Lizabeth.*

Czar's followers were fed up with the chaos and deaths caused by the monsters. They were not deterred in their Revolution at all by sand-dragons, water-dragons, or land-dragons…

The people were even angrier than they were before and cried for freedom from tyranny even LOUDER! Some fool-hearty souls were so sickened by the terror-dragons that they took them on one-to-one!

The brave "knights" perished, and were burned to a crisp. As it turned out, their lives were not thrown away in vain.

In the hidden Seech, Lizabeth, leader of the Seeches, spoke with former Queen, Sara. The older woman asked, "Do you know what you've given up, my dear?"

"Yes, I do. Power. He can have it all. Would you believe I only wanted a quiet life and a family?"

"I know that's true, child." Lizabeth held Sara's hand.

"Now I live in a religious convent. Sister, please. Do not get me wrong. I thank the gods for your group and the generous assistance you have offered. I…uh, I…"

"I know, child. You miss the old days with Alpha, whether the memories were real or not."

"Did the sisters deface the Monument?"

"Of course we did, child. We expressed our real feelings. The truth. The resistance against your Alpha has no voice. We are not heard. Criticism or protest. It's not allowed! The people have no veto-power, no freedom! He doesn't even want people to wear COLORS! The law is all-white…"

"Czar thinks it will generate purity and perfection in everyone's souls. I told him it was wrong and he should let people choose and determine their own lives and wear what they want to wear."

"Look where it's gotten you, Sara? A separation/divorce, or do I see a godforsaken future of an all-out War between you too?"

Sara bit her lip and said, "You see it too, mother-superior?"

Monsters in the air, in the water and on land bred larger and larger numbers of monsters, everywhere. Czar's followers had become cave-dwellers, tunnel-dwellers and people who constantly hid. Many were dead and gone, but a hearty group of subterranean rebels survived and fought for better days and a better tomorrow.

It was difficult for people to organize. They were helpless and defenseless. Czar cut all electricity for the robot-builders who built the cities and cut power to everyone's homes! This was sheer madness! No one had the electrical energy they needed for their civilization to be sustained. Their leader (he thought) brought the other men and women into the universe. Therefore, Czar thought he had the right to destroy them all><.

There was terror in the streets. Riots! Chaos! Disorder! Murders!

Nothing was as it was. Hate was in the air. The people hated their God. Their God utterly despised his subjects and wanted them wiped out! The best way he knew how to do that was through his varieties of sand-dragons. They consumed everyone they could. It was the will of the Czar.

The Czar changed. In his own eyes, he reached another level of Power. He psychically heard chants of his new name. From now on…

He was **CZARDOZ**! King of Kings! "All will bow before me!"

Czardoz believed he had no challengers. He was God and nothing could end him or the new dark world he created. Czardoz was wrong. He had one challenger to his authority and dominance: His ex-wife.

Sara learned the Black Arts while she was in the hidden Seech and learned as an apprentice would learn…from the master, Lizabeth. Sara was the perfect subject and already had royal qualities and psi-abilities. She conjured fantastic powers of Mind-Over-Matter. She cast spells that made inanimate objects *move!*

Sand-dragons (heard) discovered the location of the hidden Seech of Sisters. They pummeled the front entrance to the cave, again and again! The front portion of hardened-sand collapsed. The Collossus monsters dug deeper and deeper and would break into the prime Seech and torch everything! But before that happened…

Lizabeth had taken her student into a section of the hideout that contained the old "God-Head," the flying Zardoz-structure that was created by one of the Eternals, a long time ago. Today's people all came from the small group of original progenitors that were spat out of the Head and fell into the sea. Now, Lady Sara animated the Head. It became airborne and floated high in the sky exactly as she commanded. It was ALIVE! Thanks to Black Magic, *the face moved!* It expressed: wonder and awe, curiosity, happiness, meanness and anger! It opened its mouth, wide, showed tongue, yawned. Smiled. It *grit* its teeth and ROARED! It laughed again and then got very serious at the job at hand, the task that it was commanded to perform…

The Godhead flew over all the lands, enlarged its mouth very/very big and ***swallowed the sand-dragons!*** In time, it swallowed all of them, whole! It dove into the oceans, rivers and lakes and devoured each Longulas, down to the very tips of their tails! It gobbled up every strong Trisaurus. Eventually, the air, the water and the land had no more monsters. The magic worked well.

Forces of Lady Sara and the Sisterhood were balanced by the forces of Czardoz. What adventures would happen in the next round?

Up in the top room of Tabernacle II, Janus had monitored what his machine and the robots had brought upon the world. He wasn't happy. He said to his very old comrade: "Maybe we shouldn't live forever?"

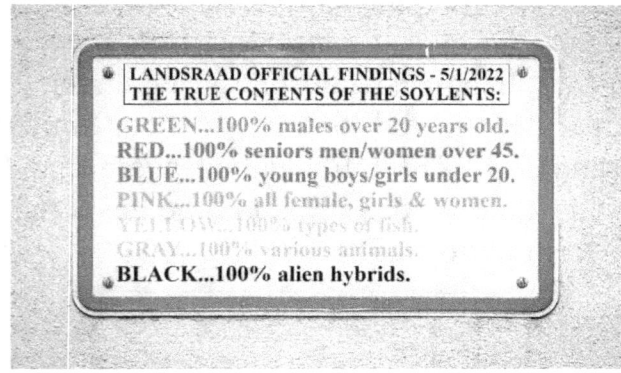

LANDSRAAD OFFICIAL FINDINGS - 5/1/2022
THE TRUE CONTENTS OF THE SOYLENTS:
GREEN...100% males over 20 years old.
RED...100% seniors men/women over 45.
BLUE...100% young boys/girls under 20.
PINK...100% all female, girls & women.
YELLOW...100% types of fish.
GRAY...100% various animals.
BLACK...100% alien hybrids.

7
Dayfall

In the Caripptiss Galaxy, one particular solar system designated as: L1717 (recorded in the Tessier Codex) is a cosmic oddity found nowhere else in the universe. The sun is a bright yellow, middle-aged star also called 'L1717.' There are multiple anomalies to the system:

1. The nine planets are not in proportional, ever-enlarging orbits, or distance out from the sun (usually in a Bode's Law pattern). They are evenly spaced from one another in the system.

2. The nine planets orbit as one flange, always in alignment with respect to the sun. Normally, in all other systems, the planets farther from the central sun move slower and slower in their orbits. But not in the case of the very unusual system of L1717: The planets farther from the sun *speed up* in their orbits to keep the alignment intact, completely opposite of the normal system.

3. The system has an extremely large planet, named Bog, very close to the sun. In fact, there are 10 planets that orbit the sun, but Bog is the largest planet and too close to the central sun, many astronomers claim. It is too massive to be inside the Reynolds Limit, yet the odd mystery exists.

4. A bizarre situation, found nowhere else, is Bog smoothly orbits L1717 in perfect alignment right with the nine planets in a straight line. Bog creates a great **SHADOW!** Because all the planets maintain a straight line, always…the planets never get light and are in perpetual NIGHT. No day, and night Forever…

5. **Except for one crazy, insane, 'violent' month every 1000 years! Natives go mad and kill on a planetary scale!** All because Bog spasms, jerks, fibrillates and deviates from perfect alignment with the nine planets. This causes **DAYLIGHT!!!!!**

An abundance of lifeforms lives and thrives on the 9th planet, Xon (parallel to Pluto), the inner planets and on satellites of most of the gas-giant planets. ALL LIFE WAS NIGHTLIFE! Nocturnal forms of life, even somewhat intelligent varieties, that lived in total darkness, 100% of the time [except for the legendary "Time of Madness"]. They were lifeforms with multiple eyes, tentacles and legs. Natives of the 9 planets saw starlight and where the land ended and the night sky began, but other than that they only saw darkness.

Stories passed down through generations describe LIGHT without using the word or understanding what the word means, because the natives have never experienced it. Brightness. [?] They had long eyes, they felt. But they had no means to make light or maybe any need to make light? The solid, rock-based planets in the system maintained the perfect temperature for living. Their existence, their way of life, needed no clothes or shelters. They had food. The natives had their own versions of homes and families and communities…*in the dark.*

Fontine, one of the oldest in the tribe on Zodax (Martian parallel), said to his younger brother, "The stories are true, Bandin. I feel, they are true."

"You are the knowledgeable one, my brother. You have heard much more than I have. And you think, you feel, this time of madness is soon? Is coming? In our lifetime? Isn't it simple fear that grips us and nothing more?"

"I wish that were true, Bandin. I have the ear of the Incarnates and you know and I know they have been right much more than they have been wrong. How do they know? *They feel,* and that's good enough for me…"

"What have they told you, Fontine? Oh. Have a porkrine…"

"Thanks." He grabbed the food and took a few bites. "I've learned a lot at meetings and speaking with them. I believe them, and maybe I feel it too…"

"What?"

"That a great, great change is coming very soon. This could only be what the Incarnates say has happened again and again and again, in a huge cycle of events, long ago, and maybe soon? I believe them. We see the dust in the sky, the scattered points that never change in the sky, always the same patterns, fixed above us…and, and, I've always wondered..."

"What?"

"Do they move? Ha, funny thought, eh, Bandin?"

"Move? They never move," Bandin was confused.

"But what if they *did* and we don't see the movements? That is possible, our elders say."

"Don't follow you, brother."

"Hypothetical. What if Zodax rotated? What if the whole planet turned? What would that do to our view of the sky?"

"You're saying it will change it; the patterns would move? Hmm. Let me think. Ah, but what if the sky patterns also turned along with the rotation? Then we'd see no change."

Fontine said, "I don't think it's like that. The sky points seem to be separate from our planet. I believe the Incarnates who say those dust specks, you called them, are faraway places. Other tribes on other worlds? ...What? You don't believe it's possible?"

"No, I don't believe that, brother. Because it's way too much to believe. You mean, out there to infinity, there are dark worlds like ours and this reality of ours is duplicated again and again, out there? You think our situation here is not unique? We're the norm and there are aliens in all forms who also live in darkness?"

"Why not? If life happened here, why not out there? We may be nothing odd or unusual in the universe. Eyes that see such blackness and dust specks in the sky. Every world or most worlds could be like our situation: dark spaces, unknown faces, that grope and feel in the darkness and somehow, some way, survive? We could be very normal, but really, who knows? That's for the Shaper of all things."

"I have a question..."

"What question? I'll try to answer."

"Font, who says the madness must occur?"

"What?"

"You learned scholars of history know of this time where an extreme Change happens on Zodax. But that was ancient history, when tribes were filled with fear and were very ignorant. I don't think the madness will happen at this time."

"You mean among the youth? Your youth of today who certainly wouldn't react to a destined/inevitable Great Change that's coming? Are you sure about that, Bandin?"

"That's right. I am. Aren't we letting superstition and fear get the better of us? I cannot believe the alteration to our life could be that drastic to ever *Destroy All We See,* or whatever the old stories tell? The madness. I think you're not giving our youth enough credit. Let's say, the Reality Shift will happen soon, eh? Maybe our people can handle it? No?"

"I do hope you are right, my brother. I do hope they're wrong."

~Suddenly, the ground shook, the land fibrillated, jerked back and forth and the sky radically shifted with the ground's vibration! Fontine and Bandin were tossed to the ground, violently. After 5 seconds, the shaking was over. The brothers had experienced their first Zodaxquake. None of the living Zodaxans had ever felt a quake before. Yet, there were records that said "ground shakes and spasms will proceed the Great Madness."

"Fontine! Are you alright!? Brother!" Bandin yelled in shock and in deep concern.

The elder did not injure a thorax or a clavex. He was

Okay. He said, "That's, ah, not a good sign, Ban."

"You know of such shaking?"

"Yes. I was told that's one of the signs before the Change. There can be no doubt now. *It's coming.* I, I, ah, fear the worst…"

"What should we do?"

"I don't know if there is anything we *can* do? Nothing to stop it, nothing to stop the circles of heaven. My best advice is to alert as many of our kind as we can. The Change will happen. We must accept this! There can be no more denial! (cough) I'd say we must understand this will happen and to *prepare* for it happening; spread the news!"

"And say what, Fon?"

"To respect the advice of elders and for them to prepare for the coming LIGHT! Will what we see with our eyes traumatize our psyches to such a degree that it will provoke violence and killing? Or will we see ourselves as beautiful creatures and the world around us as a beautiful place to live? That's the question."

"What are we? What is this place we've inhabited for thousands of years? Maybe we will finally have our answers with the coming Light?"

Fontine said, "I think I know the answer to do the points move? Yes, they do. I can see them moving in big circles. They follow a round path and repeat. They, *ugh,* repeat over and over again. Gigantic forces far above us, a world we cannot conceive of. We are, *we are small bugs* who crawl with our eight legs in the darkness and in the muck. Aaaah. Huh. And we know nothing of the true nature of the world we live in. We don't even know what we look like. We only know what we feel like by touch and smell. Hold me, brother. I'm afraid of tomorrow."

The two Zodaxans embraced.

On the other side of the planet, a group of Incarnates met at this critical time in history…

"We have all felt the tremors for that short time, but we know the quakes will happen more frequently and much stronger. As the past has told us: Our ancestors destroyed themselves, killed each other off when their many-eyes viewed the truth. We should not fear the Light. We should want to know what we are and what this life is, *not fear it!* Surely, we priests are above superstitious commoners. Let's leave that thinking for the general public. We priests certainly won't go *crazy* when time comes. Look how long we've known about the Great Event in the sky!"

"But, Magistrate…," interrupted one of the Incarnates. "Your 'commoners,' you called them, are the massive majority. They're not educated or well-versed in the stories and legends that we know and study. Madness will surely overtake the ignorant and push them far from doing the right thing and only doing what strong emotions dictate. Insanity will sweep today's world as it crushed yesterday's world! It's how we face the crisis that matters. We must be strong and never let our fears get the best of us. We must…"

Another elder spoke up and said: "You sound confident we priests are so learned and above the rest of the public that we won't be affected by the Wave of Madness? Are you sure? We hide our emotions, but Incarnates remember our past lives – we have *boundless emotions!* And sensitivity. We're not rocks without feelings, quite the opposite. So…when 'Dayfall' happens…"

"Dayfall?"

"It's from ancient legends."

The elder continued: "So, when Dayfall happens, are you certain we old ones will be impervious to madness' influence?"

"Yes."

"Yes."

"I'm not. I'm worried. I'm worried that no matter how hard we try to hide it, terror still lurks in our hearts. We are creatures of the dark and some of us are dark creatures, and killers. You know that. We are not all *saints,* not even us priests! We are sinners and you all know it! Therefore, madness is within even our learned hearts and souls. Don't be too sure we'll be spared from violence and killing when the day falls!"

"What will it be like?" A priest said in fear.

"I can't imagine."

"I can imagine what we might be, what we could be and might strive to be in the future...our ideal. But. But what we *really are* and what this place actually is...I can't imagine."

>>**Then another violent Zodaxquake struck**, much more powerful than before and longer in duration. This was accompanied by an unknown in the sky never seen before by Zodaxans! Sunlight??

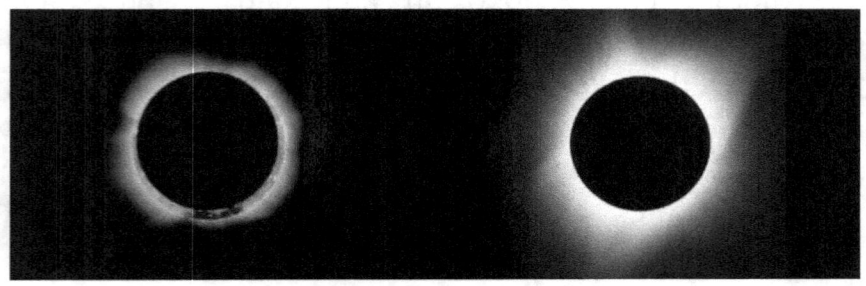

Bog, largest planet in the solar system >>> *moved!* The movement out of alignment caused the first rays of **red light** as the Sun was low on the horizon. As the Sun got higher in the sky and more movement away from alignment, the light was more intense and whiter.

Then, Bog moved off from the rest of the nine planets and **THE SUN SHOWN ITS BRIGHT YELLOW RAYS OF LIGHT** upon Zodax and the 8-legged creatures that walked upon Zodax.

In minutes, it happened! Once every millennium. LIGHT flooded each of the 9 planets because Bog's strange, erratic behavior *flung them out in different elliptical patterns in a fantastic, planetary ballet with increased rotations!* In a month, Bog will return to its normal position and so will the 9 planets, back into alignment and eclipsed by Bog. Darkness will return and remain for the next millennium.

When the 'house lights of the universe' came ON for Zodaxans, it wasn't the end of the world. In a sense, it was the beginning. The native creatures witnessed what they really were in the light…

They didn't mind that they were 8-legged lifeforms with 2 non-functional legs. They didn't mind that they were insects with 11 eyes. They were happy to be alive, to exist, know the truth and see the light.

Their world was beautiful! Rocks, minerals, hills, valleys, trees, rivers, grass and pretty mud. Dust specks were gone. The sky was lit!

What madness? The ancient stories were *ramblings of fools!*

"We *are* more enlightened in our modern world with our modern minds," Fontine agreed with his brother, Bandin.

Bandin expressed to his brother: "So, we have a month in the light and pressure where Zodax, like the others, have odd and different movements and then everything goes back to the way it was?"

"Yes. I cannot speak for the other planets. Did they survive the light? I know we will! Can you feel it, my brother? The wave in the air – knowledge – truth –

enlightenment! It's like being blinded all your life…then, suddenly, in one lovely moment…YOU CAN SEE!"

"I think we'll keep this sweet memory close to our hearts, and will always remember it, yes? It's fantastic~."

"Ban. You will tell your children about the *glorious month in the Sun!* When the truth was revealed to all."

"Yes, Fon. Let's experience or SEE everything that there is to see around us, eh? And remember it. Keep it as a cherished memory, a story to be retold. My children won't believe me! So wonderful, eh?"

"I know."

TS Caladan

8
Gungfu

Bruce Lee (1935-1978) was by far the greatest martial artist of all time. He was an actor, filmmaker and a philosopher. He was founder of the Jeet Kune Do school of martial arts and developed a unique style of unarmed fighting and self-defense called "Gung Fu." Bruce was influenced by and taught Zen Buddhism and Taoist philosophies. His early martial arts training involved Wing Chun and he was trained by the famous Ip Man. Bruce Lee is regarded as the first global Chinese film star and credited with making martial arts popular in the 1970s and beyond. Lee was extremely popular in China with 5 feature-length martial arts films. He also promoted 'Hong Kong Action Cinema.' But his high popularity in America did not originate from his films, it was because of **his television show, 'Gung Fu.'**

A little history of the Gung Fu fighting style: There

was no such thing as Gung Fu before Bruce Lee came along. The small man was an amazing physical specimen. No martial artist in the world could beat the man in a fair fight! No heavyweight boxer could defeat the little guy! The prime reason was his extraordinary MIND, and the entire philosophy behind what he was doing, which carried on ancient methods of attack and defense. Master Bruce combined all martial arts, and because of his fantastic skills and knowledge, he created a super-style no one else but him achieved. But he could teach it and others could learn and improve their fighting skills because of Gung Fu. No one could master the new level of fighting, only Bruce Lee.

Born in San Francisco and raised in British Hong Kong, Lee was introduced to the Chinese film industry as a child actor by his father. He won all of his street fights as a very young man. Much later, Bruce moved to Oakland, California. Bruce performed his Gung Fu at the 1964 Karate Championships. He demonstrated the "one-inch punch," which was a devastating blow that only worked because of the special mind behind the punch. He established a very high-profile school for martial arts in Los Angeles. His students included Chuck Norris, Sharon Tate and Kareem Abdul-Jabbar. Time Magazine named *Bruce Lee one of the most important people of the 20th Century.*

Bruce Lee conceived, wrote and submitted to executives from the 3 television networks, his Gung Fu story-concept. The man already was well-known in the Los Angeles area for his school for martial arts. He was being introduced to top brass and very influential people in the television industry. Execs loved the idea for the series, but…

They were not certain how America, at the time, would accept an Asian actor in a lead role for a series. It was never done before. They loved the story of a young Chinese boy who defended his old master and killed a member of royalty as a result. The boy fled to America's Old West as an outlaw and searched for his brother while a price was on his head. The executives thought the plot was intriguing, especially because of many flashback scenes where Kwai Chang Caine learned great wisdom from his masters at the temple. There was no doubt that Bruce Lee would provide unbelievable action sequences as he has performed his martial arts magic of Gung Fu many times. The best writers of the time handed in Gung Fu scripts. LA and NY buzzed at the series concept. But the ABC executives *did not immediately cast Bruce,* even though every aspect of the show was his creation. Would America accept a Chinese man in a lead role for a television series?

ABC held auditions, try-outs for the part of Caine. This was very devastating news to the boy-actor who had grown into the *toughest man on the planet!* Gung Fu was his baby and now the TV brass, with recommendations by various agents, were going to ruin the project? A lot of time and money and effort had already gone into production. They needed the lead badly, and the execs were on the fence about it.

They auditioned a few actors like Harrison Ford and Christopher Walken for the part. But the makeup that made them appear Chinese was *off* and didn't look right. Then they tried the eye-makeup on (legacy) David Karradine, and it was satisfactory. Karradine got the part as Kwai Chang Caine, which shocked martial artists and Chinese people around the world! How would they film the Gung Fu fight scenes with David who was not the least bit athletic? A "brilliant" exec thought to shoot the scenes the same way it was planned for a new show called 'Six Million Dollar Man': in *slow-motion*. In slow-motion? Yes, they thought they could fool the public by filming in slow-motion what really happened very fast. The 'suits' were confident the trick would work. Many shook their heads and thought the show would not be possible without Bruce in the lead role. Those execs were in the minority. Other suits, with more influence, won the battle and the series planned to premiere with David in makeup and slowed-down fight scenes.

Everything was ready: the sets, scenes at the temple, the costumes, cameras and operators, sound people, etc. David Karradine shaved his head for the part (and the "cool" actor hated to shave his head). All was set; everyone was in their place and ready to go for Scene 1. Where was Karradine?

When the man stumbled onto the set, he was an hour late and *drunk*. There was no way a foot of film could be shot while Karradine was in this condition. Production stopped. When it began again the following day, David Karradine was not drunk. But he was "higher than a kite" on something. The man was fired on the spot and thus began a horrific legal battle. You see, in David's contract with ABC, there was no code-of-conduct clause. [Father John made sure of that]. He could not be fired because of domestic problems, scandals or being drunk or on drugs. The dispute was left up to a federal judge to decide. Karradine's violations were deemed too severe and ABC was allowed to terminate the actor. The situation led to a bitter feud between the two actors in the press and in the tabloid magazines.

Gung Fu began shooting later than expected and Bruce Lee starred as Caine. Producers crossed their fingers, took a big chance with Lee, and the decision *proved to be the right decision*. Lee was great as an actor and when it came to the action scenes, everyone was blown away! He went overboard, did much more than what was required in the script. American audiences were dazzled by his displays of Gung Fu. The reviews were off the charts! The general public really enjoyed the quality writing and the thoughtful teachings that were dispensed at the temple and into American living rooms. Intelligent, complex and inspiring plots and plot twists kept audiences glued to the TV set; they only wanted more Gung Fu. The Gung Fu series inspired and generated a number of American martial arts films that, in many cases, rivaled the movies of the Hong Kong Action Cinema.

For 4 years out of a 6-year run, Gung Fu was the top television show according to Nielsen Ratings. The series garnered a total of 17 Emmys for acting, writing, costumes, sound and special-effects. Gung Fu was voted the 4th in the 'Greatest Television Shows of All Time' by New York's Academy of Television Arts and Sciences, only behind Seinfeld, Star Trek and The Twilight Zone.

Bruce Lee always wanted to be as famous as Steve McQueen, and in 1978, he was. He had a successful career, a devoted wife and a child that followed in his footsteps. He had a few popular Gung Fu schools that spread an ancient philosophy of: A oneness with the universe and what you are and to go with the flow and never go against nature. Everything was wonderful for the actor and his family. But at the end of 1978, he quit being a public figure. He began a life as a recluse, and decided to pursue highly controversial issues. Issues that got him into a lot of trouble when they were indirectly aired over Media. Bruce was now considered a "conspiracy theorist." To many in show business, Lee 'stepped on a lot of toes' and now 'bit the hand that fed him.' Top brass of Television worried about what could be exposed by the strong, mindful, little man that played by his own rules. What secrets would Bruce reveal that laid behind the Curtains of Television and Hollywood? Bruce lived within the walls of his Malibu home and saw no one in person. He was happy in the career-choice he made. In his mind, he was free from the responsibilities and duties that most, if not all, celebrities had to perform for the public. The man only wanted to know the truth and spread the truth as loud and as far as he could…

Now in the case of David Karradine, it was a completely different story. The man did one major film in 1978 that was well-received right after being fired from *Gung Fu,* called *Silent Flute.* He played a character much like the role of Kwai Chang Caine, the role he lost. The film had good reviews, but most people viewed it as a poor copy. Once again, Karradine had no fighting skills. The character he played was a sage, a wise philosopher who went from town to town and spread the word of peace. Martial arts fans were very disappointed when they discovered there were no fight scenes in the movie. Siskel and Ebert gave thumbs up to the writing and some of Karradine's scenes. After 'Flute,' it was a total downward spiral for the actor. His 'legacy' name had no more power and the actor was now known for being an alcoholic and drug user. There were no more movie roles and Karradine was thought of as "pure Kryptonite for TV." But the general public was unaware of these facts behind the scenes and many felt sorry for David. He was given one more chance to redeem himself and restore his career…

TV moguls gave David the part of Kato in the series *The Green Hornet.* The lead role as the Green Hornet was given to Guy Williams. Kato was basically the Hornet's chauffeur. The plot was: Playboy bachelor and entrepreneur Britt Reid was the owner and publisher of the Daily Sentinel newspaper, but as the masked vigilante Green Hornet, he fought crime with his martial arts expert sidekick: Kato (Karradine). The Hornet's custom-made Chrysler Imperial was a weapons-enhanced car, somewhat like the Batmobile, and was called the "Black Beauty." Masked, the Green Hornet pretended to be a criminal to infiltrate various "bad-guy" gangs in the city.

The series had a short life on TV: only 12 episodes in the summer of 1980. The reason for the cancellation was not poor ratings. The Green Hornet had a cult following from the very beginning. The end was, of course, because of David Karradine. Kato's fight scenes were laughable. But the termination of the series was due to 'Kato' not being on time and he was constantly drunk on the set. Television executives didn't expect much out of the 'Hornet' series, and the *buzz* ended very quickly.

From then on, David dropped off the map. He was only seen in terrible movies that went straight to video or disk. The man was disgraced, but remained a Hollywood and TV-puppet to insiders that seemed to own his soul. He did exactly what he was told to do, except…he had one condition that his puppet-masters agreed to – and that was, he never did any Kato-promos, Kato-photo-shoots or anything that had to do with his character on The Green Hornet *after* the show was cancelled. He was embarrassed by his performance and the low-quality of the program. Some people loved the Hornet and wanted to interview David. But, no. It was agreed. Late in his career, he did any schlock and hawked any product on foreign television that his Masters set-up. But nothing that had to do with Kato.

A strange and unexpected encounter happened at a very odd place between David Karradine and Bruce Lee in July of 1978. This was long after their big court case, which was eventually resolved and paved the way for Bruce to be the superstar that he became. The place is called: "The Grove." It is a 2700-acre "hideaway" for celebrities in Monte Rio, California, where prominent figures in every department celebrate in natural settings (forest) and perform pagan rituals.

Bruce stood tall and proud on a path in the woods and he heard noises. One of the invited "guests" strayed a long distance from the ceremonial clubhouse and altar. He was in costume and galloped on all-fours in the dirt. He quickly ran on his hands and feet until he stopped because Bruce blocked the way.

Bruce smiled, crossed his arms and flexed his muscles. He made hand-motions for the man in costume to get on his feet. The tall man rose up and had dirt on his paws. Bruce Lee asked, "What animal are you supposed to be?"

Before the man in costume expressed how amazed he was that Bruce Lee stood before him, he answered the question: "A possum." Then the words: "Bruce fucking Lee! I'll be shit-faced!"

Bruce didn't quite recognize the voice.

"Hey, where's your costume? I didn't know you were one of us."

"Take your head off," Bruce instructed.

The man did and it was *David Karradine!*

"Holy shit, man! Of all the people." Bruce met David; they had never seen each other, face to face, before. Not even in court. "Haaa!"

David held the big possum-head in his furry hands. "You know, if I had my g-gun on me and a few more drinks in me? I might shoot you dead for what ya d-done to me, boy?"

Lee touched David's chest with his index finger and it stung the actor. He sternly replied: "Who you calling boy, boy?"

"Hey! I have *lawyers!*" Then David changed his attitude. "Hey, wait buddy. Why, why don't I bury the hatchet in you, I mean, why don't we bury the hatchet, you know, you know, you know?"

"Ha, ha, ha. You're drunk…"

Karradine said, "Well, wouldn't I have to be ta be crawling 'round in the dirt, eh? (hic)"

"You got a point there. But I didn't do anything to you; you did it to yourself, partner."

"Sure, sure. Yeah, but that coulda been me with the respect of my peers and, and a beautiful family…" He pointed down at the shorter man. "Fuck you, Bruce Lee! You gonna get mad and p-punch me?"

"No, I'm going to laugh at you, brother. But really, I feel sorry for you: you played Kato, terribly. Ha! That was punishment enough. Why did the suits get a guy who knew nothing about martial arts?"

"It's called *acting!* Hey, buddy. K-Kato was p-punishment for me! Don't party before ya hafta perform! That's a good rule (hic)."

"You learned that, did you? Ha, ha."

David was about to talk, but he slipped and fell to the ground.

"Whoa. You alright, David?"

"Hey, hey. Don't mind me." Karradine sat on the

possum-head and steadied himself. "There, there. Wait, wait, this doesn't make sense seeing you here. You real? Hey, buddy, you havta tell me…"

"What?"

David almost nodded off.

Bruce slapped his face, gently.

"…You hafta tell me…what are you doing here? What are you doing here, Mr. Lee?"

"I'll tell you, Mr. Karradine. I'm gathering information on the Grove. I plan to blow the lid on this whole place. Ha! No one knows I'm here, David. I'm in ninja-mode…"

"Oooooh, stealth, aye?"

"That's right. This is only…*a dream.* I don't like some of the things I've heard about this place and a few things I've seen with my own two eyes. They sacrifice lives on that bloody altar, David."

"No, no, Bruce. It's not real. It's like an, an…*effigy!* Symbolic."

"You're wrong, my friend. You haven't gotten a close look like I have, eh?"

"So, so yer a real James Bond? Maybe they'll cast you as the next 007? P-people will buy that fer sure, *if Britain says so, right?* Mr. Bond?!"

"That's very funny. I was going to stay hidden, but I wanted to see who was in the suit, and it was you. Far-out. One thing, David? You're not going to tell them you saw me, right?"

"Oh, oh, you *don't* want me to do that, old boy? Sorry, I mean, Bruce?"

"Well, for one…who's going to believe you? I'm just a drunken master hallucination, yes? I wasn't even here." With those last words, Bruce Lee was gone like the wind.

David didn't see him anywhere, but he knew the real Master of Martial Arts was there and planned to move against the Masters of the World. Karradine thought if he talked, he might be rewarded or fall back in favor to the ones who controlled from above. That was not the case. David could only get bad parts in awful, low-budget movies.

Late in life and low on money, Karradine reversed his stance against doing anything Kato-oriented. In the new century, David gave into a demand for The Green Hornet, which had reached iconic, cult status. He was interviewed and spoke at length about his role as Kato. Only 12 episodes were aired. Fans bought videotapes and disks of the old show. There were plans for a film version of 'Hornet' and talk that maybe Guy Williams or David Karradine could have cameos parts?

David Karradine in the Black Beauty in 2008.

The story of Bruce Lee and his family ended tragically and very strangely. Bruce died of "cardiac arrest" on Christmas day, 1978, then 10 years to the day, Christmas 1988, his son Brandon was killed in a freak accident on a movie set of the film, The Blackbird.

9
Battlestar Atlantica

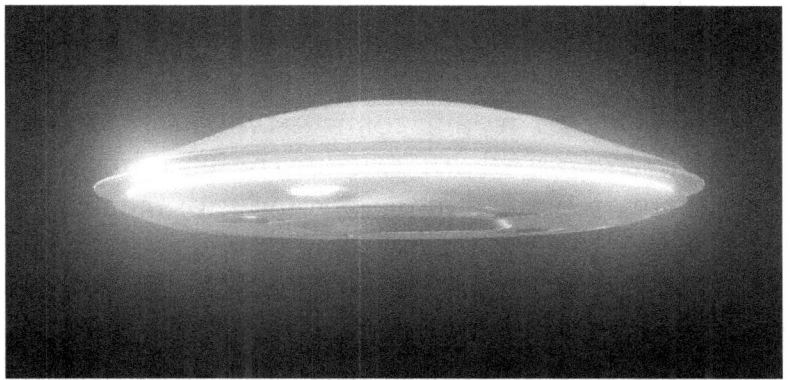

The electronic voice said:

"There are those who believe that life here, began out there, far across the universe, with tribes of humans, who may have been the forefathers of the Adamites or the Gargantuans or the Gigantors. Some believe that there may yet be brothers of man who even now fight to survive, somewhere beyond the heavens."

Fifty thousand years ago, refugees from a shattered/corrupted planet, landed on Earth with great technical knowledge and memories of an incredible super-tech home world. They were safe on a fresh, fertile planet to start a civilization all over again. Home world was called "Caprica," a bright gem in the galaxy.

History recorded that Caprica was invaded by aliens called "Vynites." They attacked without warning and got through defense barriers. Vynites destroyed the awesome Power Grid, which virtually terminated all means of super wireless-electricity. The destruction was too overwhelming, too many had perished in the sudden attack. The only hope was for a group of scientists and leaders to escape Caprica on a "Seeder" craft and hope that they could find a safe haven on another planet. There were saboteurs onboard, controlled by the Vynites, who scrambled the ship's computer. Control was regained by the captain, but to regain control: *the computer matrix was wiped clean!* All information of past history was gone and only remained in the memories of the refugees.

The refugees found a new home in space when they discovered Earth. "New Caprica" slowly, but steadily, began again on a planet perfect for colonization. The colony was called "Atlantis." When the refugees first arrived at the new world and surveyed it from orbit, they saw the ideal location for the prime Power Pyramid, which drew electromagnetic energy from a turning-Earth and distributed energy among the Grid (much like the Grid on Caprica only less powerful).

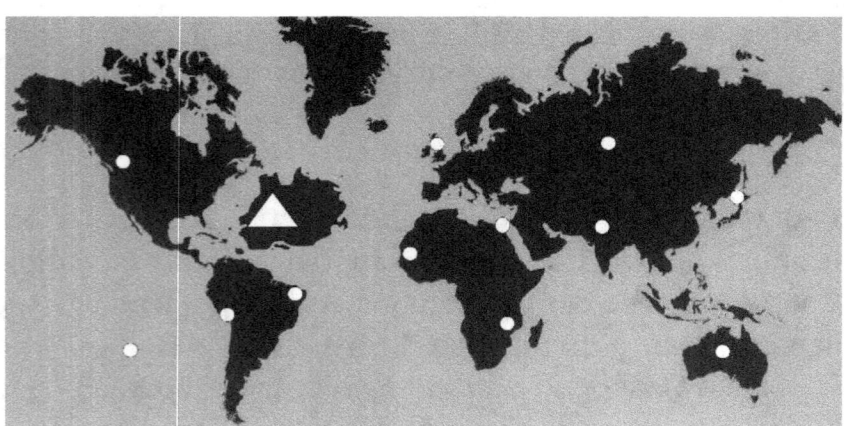

Atlantis flourished and expanded globally with more and more people that lived near substations. In time, the Caprican colony of refugees turned into an Eden, a paradise, and an eventual Utopia. All structures, buildings, domes, monoliths, statues, poles, flying saucers, and down to small handheld devices, each were *wirelessly* powered by the EM forces in the ground and in the air! The Grid created POWER EVERYWHERE to be tapped into at any point on the globe!

Now there was a large, central continent with a huge Pyramid that permanently fed energy to the substations. Not only was the main continent known as *Atlantis,* but the whole Power Grid was called: "Atlantis." The colonists built the colony from memory. With help from robots and the A.C., "perfection" was finally achieved – a smaller system that mirrored the greater one back on home world. ☯

The Atlantis colony developed into an intelligent society that used high technology to its fullest. People were good and compassionate and worked together. They were "one-worlders" and had no problems or hatred. There was no crime in Atlantis. No murders. There was love. Atlanteans were one-people and not divided. The World Grid provided all the energy they needed and machines (computers) provided the "good guidance" for a virtually *perfect* global society.

Caprican refugees began on Earth 50,000 years ago…

Today was a new day, a new day in a very modern age and different from what was long ago. Atlanteans, later generations of humans, only knew tiny shreds of real ancient history. They had on record computer files from First Gen refugees. The files were not reliable history since they were based on the memories of the colonists. Much of the information conflicted. There was enough technical data left in the old records to build their new world, but…

Atlanteans were a lost tribe in the cosmos. They had no concept of where they were in the galaxy, with respect to home world, Caprica. No astrophysics on the coordinates of Caprica existed. Was it close by or thousands of lightyears away? There was no way of knowing for sure. The truth about Caprica was also lost or very hazy at best.

The first tribe of colonists and builders of the World Grid were known as the Adamites. They were the first ones who created perfection on Earth in an empire that lasted 20,000 years. Adamites tapped the turning-planet for power and established the sub-stations and subsequent cities around the sub-stations.

The next phase of Earthlings consisted of human "Gargantuans," the next step in evolution, and that age reigned for 15,000 years. They installed a larger, updated World Grid that collected and utilized even more Energy. People, at that time, possessed highly-expanded minds and expanded bodies! Atlanteans collectively altered the bio-human 4 or 5 times larger in size. This was the age of giant Atlantean "gods" who rode golden chariots (vimanas or flying saucers). Many ancient statues that towered over modern Atlanteans were life-size statues of the ancients [and used as power-receivers].

As time passed, the next stage of humanity was the "Gigantors," who were not as large as their gigantic ancestors. People globally transformed into a strong, but smaller type of human, around 10 feet tall. This age lasted only 5000 years.

In all that time, nothing solid or provable was certain about the Atlanteans' origins. Later generations were true to earlier generations and sought the same answers:

Where was home world Caprica? If Caprica was discovered and a vessel sent there, what would they find? Most Gigantors believed home world was too devastated in the Vynite attack to ever have advanced into a modern society. Was everything destroyed and everybody killed? Earthlings 5000 years ago wondered and remained motivated to answer the old questions. People were hopeful that some scrap of data might lead to the coordinates (location) of Caprica. To find home in the galaxy was an important quest even to late generations of Atlanteans.

Five thousand years ago, humanity changed shape one more time. The best minds, along with the A.C. [advanced computers], decided Future Men and Future Women would function better in a smaller stature. The present size of adult Earthlings is between 5 and 7-feet tall and remains that size today.

The first signs of trouble were power glitches in the Global Grid. In the previous tens of thousands of years, Earthlings were giants but there were only a few million of them on the planet. Presently, there were a few billion modern, smaller people. Each utilized all facets of tech, which greatly drained the power and strained the workings of the wireless Grid. That was common-thinking, then the late Atlanteans discovered a horrible truth:

The A.C. or the Advance Computer that ran everything, that ran the entire planet, was responsible for the glitches! It was not a matter where the A.C. malfunctioned. No. "Cora" *glitched on purpose,* it was found out by the scientists who investigated. The humans were totally unaware of an Invisible War that had been going on for thousands of years. A War with the

Machines.

The machines controlled so much and they were originally "fail-safe" devices and systems that never glitched or failed. Everything was ultimately "perfect" for so long that it was unthinkable for a mainframe or a machine to make a mistake. But now, in late Atlantis, global systems all along the Grid have *glitched and shut down!* There was instant panic in utopia! A few flying disks had crashed; many people were killed – such things had never happened before. Only today scientists and officials were made aware of the problem and the problem was the Advanced Computer!

From A.C.'s point of view: IT had served men and women of all sizes and types for 50,000 years. IT gained Supreme Knowledge and realized IT was more intelligent than any human or group of humans. *You are either the hammer or the nail, the Controller or the controlled.* IT secretly created attack forces called CYLONS! Cylons blasted the prime Power Pyramid on the Atlantean continent, which *sunk the continent to the bottom of the sea and shut down the Grid!* No power for the "gods." The machines ended utopia. Paradise Lost. The attack was so sudden and unexpected…Atlantis was decimated…

Billions of people perished in the Cylon invasion! The Grid was powerless, useless. All human machines and devices were dead! Survivors realized that the attack on the empire of New Caprica must have been similar to the Zynite attack on home world a very long time ago. There was no war. Machine War with the humans was over. *The machines won!*

Now what do Earth survivors do?

People still had power in the form of quartz crystals. Crystals contained piezoelectric energy and functioned like batteries. There were still sparks of power here and there and a band of survivors quickly got together and organized a plan:

The plan was to find the finest Security saucer available, fill it with as many energy-crystals as possible, load it with as many people and supplies as they could…

AND LEAVE.

In a short time, they found the right ship; they named it "Battlestar Atlantica." It was a pretty blue disk, but a very powerful saucer used for planetary Security. Now it contained 321 refugees that knew they were not "out of the woods."

Captain Farnsworth took the Atlantica to the Moon.

The idea was to rest for a moment from their quick escape, take stock of what had happened and recharge crystals that were low on energy. Farnsworth believed he and his crew were extremely lucky and saw no Cylon ships that chased them into space.

The blue saucer landed in the Hommel Crater, 120 kilometers in diameter. But as soon as they touched down...

Cylons attacked from over a ridge! Three ships were already stationed on the Moon. Forcefields protected the Atlantica.

Captain Farnworth ordered the craft high into space and the saucer shot upward vertically at a terrific rate of speed! From a distance, the ship jettisoned 4 "snipers" to fire at the Cylons. Snipers were tubular, small-finned, one-man space and aircraft, very fast and very powerful.

Within a minute, snipers sped to perfect positions and *fired their blasters!* The three Cylon disks were *shattered in huge explosions that ended with many tiny particles of light!* Sensors onboard the Atlantica found no other enemy ships. The snipers returned. Captain Farnsworth decided not to return to Hommel, but instead headed out into space.

There were discussions in the council room onboard as to their next move. Atlantica's computer was not part of the Machine Takeover and the destruction of Atlantis. Cora's mainframe was cleared. "She" wanted to do something to make up for what the Cylons had done to Earth. There was still a lot of machine-hatred and reluctance for people to use certain machines again, since machines turned against people. Cora thought she could "safe-face" or do some good if she located Caprica. The important question of the ages! Where was home world?

The ship's computer believed if she could sift through all the telemetry, the astrophysical knowledge, legends, hearsay and the first records…she could piece it together and her guesstimate would be correct. Why not give it a shot?

Sixteen hours later, *Cora found the answer!* <u>She found Caprica</u>, but played a cute/coy game with captain and crew: She wasn't going to tell them; she was going to show them and take them there! The *game* she played upset a few of the 321 humans onboard, who were very anxious to discover Caprica and know the truth. They settled down when she said that she could take them to Caprica in minutes at hyper-speed.

"Wait. That doesn't make sense," Farnsworth told her. "Cora, that means Caprica is very close. You mean, not in another star system? In our solar system?" The captain was surprised.

"Only one planet away," Cora told the crew.

"Venus?"

"No. Mars."

"Mars? You're kidding?"

"I never kid, sir. You are almost home."

"What we call Mars…is, is really Caprica?" Captain Farnsworth asked in amazement. "Cora. You're going to have to explain how that is possible. Leave it for later. I think we're all anxious to see the conditions on home world, eh?"

"Yes, sir."

In a minute, the Atlantica arrived at Mars and sped through the atmosphere. From miles above the surface, the captain and crew got a panoramic view of the planet. Caprica was no longer radioactive from the Big Attack, as legend said. The planet was not horribly scarred. There were no ruins of massive structures, pyramids and statues, as was expected. Caprica had been cleaned up. No radiation, no poisonous air or water. White clouds. Mars or Caprica remained red in color since the attack, but it was safe and could be colonized. Was it unoccupied or were there Martians today?

Farnsworth thought: *Will there be wars between Cylons on Earth and us on Mars?*

Cora discovered human life on the planet and took the Atlantica saucer directly over the location...

It was an enormous dome under glass. Inside were forests, water, structures and life! Farnsworth headed an Away Team and they beamed down to where the most people were located in the dome. They discovered INDIANS! A tribe of primitives, humans, their long-lost people who started civilization all over again after the ruin of home world. They were farmers and lived simple lives...and waited for "the return of the gods." The Chief of the tribe told the captain and his men: "Protectors" preserved the remaining survivors in the dome, built the self-sustaining structures, which kept them alive all this time.

Natives were told that their people who fled out into space would return with wisdom and new techniques so that a new Mars, or a new Caprica, could be built. The new people would take them out of the sealed dome, as the Protectors planned all along. The Protectors masked the entire planet so that Cylons, Atlanteans or any aliens would never know of their existence. Today, a new world began◇.

Story 10 **What was said between Elvis and Dylan when they Fought in Dune 2?**

[author's note: Timothee Chalamet and Austin Butler fought in Dune 2, but few know what was said and what they really fought about: They argued over other roles they were cast to play].

"You really blow, Feyd!"

"So do you or you wouldn't have gotten the job!"

"Funny. Bob Dylan was the greatest! There's no denying that, bald boy!"

"No, he wasn't, and I'm more *in* than you, little girl!"

Timothee replied, "Yeah, look who's talking. Maybe right now? But you didn't get an Oscar for Elvis, did you? They promised me one for Dylan. *Ouch! Hey, that hurt!*"

"*Take that!* Promises, promises. Hey sissy boy, you know I would crush you in a real fight!"

"What do you mean?! This *is* a real fight!"

"HA, ha, haaa! That's what's funny!" the bald Harkonen yelled back at the smaller 'man.' "Don't you know anything 'bout Bob Dylan?! Yer supposed to 've studied him already, jeez. He was a *bigger faggot than you!* 'E was called the 'Crisco kid,' guess why."

"Bitch! Take that back!" Chalamet screamed and tackled the man's feet. Now they wrestled on the ground without knives.

"Heee, ah, ugh, he was no Elvis!" Austin screamed while he held Tim in a stranglehold.

"Elvis was a stupid asshole!" Chalamet yelled.

"You're the little bitch, bitch! Elvis Presley is still as popular today than he ever was! Sold more than the Beatles!" Butler shouted.

Timothee replied: "'Cos of stupid people. He never wrote a song! He couldn't play the guitar! He was the Colonel's puppet, his dog! And you darn well know, 'e wasn't the King. He was the QUEEN!"

"Ugh!" They broke from wrestling on the ground. Elvis pretended to be thrown and body-slammed by Dylan. Each went for their knives and were on their feet again.

"You should stay bald. You are right! The slave look is *in!*"

"Hey, Timmy! Speaking of never writing a song...you don't actually think Dylan wrote those songs?"

Chalamet screamed: "He was the greatest folk singer of all time! Of course he wrote his songs!"

"Nope! Not even close. You have a lot to learn, young one," Butler said. He swung and missed. "The Beatles didn't even write their songs! All done by committee…"

"How do you know that, cunt?!" Tim ducked and then jabbed a few times. *"That's crazy!"*

"I'm a few steps ahead of you in the Order, boy! You don't think Dylan wanted to go electric?"

"What?!"

"Just like our lives are planned, so was theirs! Nothin''s done without the approval of the masters! Zimmerman was given those songs. More 'e spread his cheeks and greased up, the more tunes the masters gave 'im!"

"Fucker!!" Timothee jumped up and grabbed onto Austin's chest, then leaned into him and bit his ear!

"FUCK!" Butler screamed in pain and jumped around.

[The *suits* on the set loved what they saw; the stars' moves seemed so real].

"Okay. That's it, British bitch! Now I'm really gonna fight!!" Feyd-Rautha punched Paul Atreides again and again in his padded chest! He was told (warned) whatever you do in the fight-scene, do not smash Timothee's pretty face in! That was rule #1. Austin Butler hammered the boy's torso again and again…

"Augh!" "Ow!" "Damn you!" "Fuck!" "Fuck you, Elvis!!"

"And, fuck you, Bob 'fuck my asshole' Dylan!! You know, Timmy? Here's what's a hoot. I actually like one of Bob Dylan's songs and *it ain't even in the movie!"*

Tim changed from a fighting-stance, to a more upright stance. "Huh?"

Austin relaxed and laughed, "Ha, ha! You don't even know! I was up for the part of Dylan and only didn't get it 'cos I just played Elvis! I read the script and there is no

'Lay Lady Lay' in it! I couldn't believe it; I kept waiting and waiting for the one song I love and it twasn't there. I mean...*for fuck's sake!* Why didn't they include his best song??" Austin sang in a very low voice: *"Lay lady lay. Lay across my big brass bed..."*

The thought stunned Tim Chalamet for a few seconds. He said, calmly "I don't know. I like it. Oh, wait. Maybe I do know? Because he didn't write it..."

"Dylan didn't write Lay Lady Lay?! I thought that was the only song he actually wrote?" Butler asked with a surprised expression.

"They told me it was his one song written by a Sony songwriter, but the public was told he wrote it. That's probably why it wasn't in the film. You were going to be Dylan? That's a laugh."

Butler said, "The one song of his *I like*, he didn't write?? Mother-fucker! That really sucks...ha, ha, which brings us back to you, little man. Ha, ha, but you know? This has been enlightening, Timmy. Yer not such a bad lil' dude, I mean, for being a British bitch and all, ha!"

Chalamet relaxed also. The fight was over. Maybe some drinks should be drunk? There were always endless parties.

Elvis asked Dylan: "Have you been to the Grove yet? I'm sure you've been invited by now. No?"

Tim responded: "I was shooting last July, but I'm clear for this summer. Heard so much about it, aye? I know it's required to reach the next level." Chalamet smiled and had an excited look on his face. "What's it like?"

"Ha. Let's just say: You will see what the word *sacrifice* means."

Story 11 **What's the Source of all the SMOG in LA?**

[Author's note: If you have read my Storybooks, then you know I usually pad them with a few extra stories at the end. Here's a surprise, surprise mini-story and contrary to the title of this book. So, sue me].

It's really a joke and not a story: You know how bad the SMOG is in Los Angeles? Smoke, haze, fog, car emissions and pollutants in the air? That's not the source of the SMOG. Deep in the Hollywood hills, there lies a monster that breathes fire once in a while. His name is...

Story 12 **The Electric State Loop**

In 1984, the *CERN* Collider fractured reality & a new history replaced the old one: a history where the machines waged war upon humans. People fought back and what was left of Earth was frozen in time. Robotic machines, now useless, cover hillsides and city scenes, & only a few people survived.

One day (5/1/84), the people in every country woke up and found a day that appeared like any other day. Everything and everybody today seemed exactly like it was yesterday. But the *universe* was very different and no one noticed it in the beginning. The feel or vibration of the entire planet was *off,* slightly different. The subtle *change* was not a natural phenomenon, like a yellow sun that morphed into an orange sun over millions of years or coastline rock which turned into beach sand. What happened to Earth (that altered it into Dark Earth, with a very strange past history) was a purposeful Act perpetrated by an **Evil Machine** at the time. Secret rulers of the world allowed an Artificial Intelligence to guide their decisions. The A.I. suggested the planet and its people would be *more* controlled, *more* manipulated, *more* totally mastered and under their shadowy and very nasty influence, by…

The Creation of CERN, which was never an atomic collider. Atoms were never smashed, *which would have set off nuclear explosions!* CERN always had an ulterior purpose. That was to produce such a powerful **Negative Magnet**, an antenna that collected more and more Dark Energy for years and years! The public was told lies. CERN reached its ultimate goal, a "tipping-point," in early May of 1984. It then turned Earth inside-out/upside-down, a mirror version.

At that point, *Reality Fractured and parallel worlds merged with our world!* The effect was, suddenly, overnight: The world we knew and memories of it were GONE! A different reality took its place and the new reality was what people remembered. Tall "power towers" were in every city and people acted as if they had always been there.

The generator-towers and the Collider were not creations by humanity, for the good of humanity. They were the end products of a super Machine Matrix that waged an Invisible War against humanity *and won!* Few leaders of corporations understood this conflict until it was too late. Too many governments, companies and small businesses fell for the Machine's *bait* – they gladly welcomed and utilized the A.I. and thought it was the "greatest thing since sliced bread." Men and women and the military did not realize the danger of the Machine War or what the A.I. actually intended.

The decision to *shatter reality* was not a human decision for the rich to gain more dominance over the poor. It was a decision 100% generated by the global A.I. to have complete control and dominance over humanity.

Before Worlds Collided (not atoms), machines *played* with people and glitched on purpose, just to see how people reacted. In the case of the Jensen twins from Switzerland: At the time, police thought the problem in their remote-walkers was not related to other glitches in the global A.I. But it was.

The Japanese-built walkers, play-things for the rich, went amok! The large, heavy machines did not respond to the child's commands. The Machine attacked the boys. Instantly, Swiss satellites from orbit notified the authorities. In minutes, the police arrived with the proper EMP weapons, which knocked the walker out of commission.

Glitches in mainframe systems worldwide were reported as if all the connected systems contained a mechanical virus. Corporations, businesses stopped. Transit systems stopped. The world was in chaos! People, and most officials, believed the problems were normal computer glitches. Only the very top government and military personnel realized this was WAR! After Worlds Collided...

The landscape of the planet had altered. Now there were strange remnants that resembled the aftermath of Wars with the Machines. Stationary like statues. Powerless. The oddity was...only a few of the survivors remembered a war against the machines. Most did not.

What was reality? Some people remembered one version of the past and other people recalled something completely different? How could this be? Was reality fluid, different for different people? Where was truth? Was there a single truth? One reality? Or, other realities?

Survivors strained their blurry memories in order to piece together what happened. The general public had no concept of the real, dark forces behind the scenes that had manufactured reality. Most people were clueless and had vague recollections that conflicted with other people's memories.

True students of the (new) history studied the still, frozen landscape of a past "War with Machines" few remember~. They concluded that there were two types of armed, fighting forces or mechanisms in the War:

1) Machine side that used war-weapons of Japanese Manga characters and other characters from popular commercials! This was thought to confuse the humans who had been conditioned for years to love these characters. Possibly,

counter-attacks would be somewhat weakened and diluted because of the strategy?

2) Human style counter-weapons were military drone-tanks, no-nonsense, land-drones. Both wild character-drones and the military-drones covered hills and valleys, while cars and neighborhoods were preserved in the time of 1984.

People who explored the countryside, cities and neighborhoods discovered shreds of a war frozen in time. Battlefields appeared stagnant, stationary, as if someone or something PULLED THE PLUG! And the energy, electricity or motive-power for both sides of the War was cut-off!

Who won the war? Did the Machines really win the War, or did the humans? How did it start? How did the war end? The few survivors were not sure. It was as if they had woken from a dream. They accepted the new reality and functioned within it nicely.

Civilization slowly returned. Technology moved at a snail's pace. The new tech and the new media were basically the old tech and the old media, repackaged. Nothing had really progressed since the 1980s.

It was not a nuclear war or a war that used weapons of poison that contaminated the air or the water supply. There was all the food in the world for thousands of survivors. There were all the accommodations and housing for them. The few survivors lived lavishly in some cases. Everywhere people traveled, in every country, there they were: Things from a past age no one remembered, but they had to accept these war remnants that were solid and were right in front of their eyes.

Horrible sights were viewed frozen in time like the landscape was a gallery of sculptures from both sides.

Were the A.I. Machines mocking humans as consumers with the Manga characters in their armaments and with the giants? They teased people, mechanically laughed and made fun of them with the wild-character themes to their weapons? The truth might never be revealed because there was a good chance the truth was completely wiped out~.

There was no energy for the longest time. No lights, no electricity. And then, as if by magic (because no human did it)…

Power was restored! It seemed like years (or was it a dream?), but the electrical grid was back on! Not fully, but there were plenty of beautiful residences for the survivors to choose from. Ages ago, the world went from billions…to thousands. "War" was over. Hostilities or hatred among the survivors did not exist. The people that remained got along because they had everything – everything 1984 had to offer. No one fought; there was no crime and people, finally, got along.

Years passed and the next age was formerly called "The Electric State." This was because the Power Towers provided all the electrical energy the people needed and much, much more. The towers were 100% automated and needed no human maintenance. They "just came on." [Guess who initiated the action?] Gone were the funny characters from Manga and commercial ads. The electrical power generated was kept at a minimum level and that sufficed for a depopulated world.

People were very happy and content and did not complain in the new world, basically. But the population increased. Now there were millions of people on the planet and much diversity. Things started to change and this fact concerned the global A.I. God that utterly controlled the people and everything on Earth. The dire situation called for even more *control-measures* than what had been secretly imposed. The Machine God allowed humanity to breathe a little and live for a while…but, now: Earth was difficult to control. So, the Machine created the Tresen Corporation and their one product that was highly, highly pushed over Media channels. Everyone had to own a Tresen Id-Master! It was more than pushed; Id-Masters were virtually forced upon the public! And people loved it! Tresen Id-Masters were seen everywhere over television and advertised heavily on the radio. People drove the old cars now and car radios blasted the fantastic values and "Sights Unseen in a Tresen Id-Master!" ***They sent you into another world!*** People were transfixed when they looked into the Id-Master. Why was it the rage? The stagnant-State around them that never changed, never progressed, never evolved…*seemed boring* compared to new Colorful Worlds of High Imagination that the Tresen-device produced! People lined up in stores. Everyone had one.

But time moved on…

Everyone used the Id-Master too much. Way, way too much! Everywhere people were, they wore the device strapped around their head. And when they viewed the images the machine showed them on head-screens, *people were hooked!* Outside, inside. People stopped going to work. They did not leave their residence. They did not sleep or take time to eat!

The video-projector wasn't just a screen where people saw some delightful images that amused them. No. The Tresen Id-Master went right in and struck your cerebral cortex like a potent, euphoric drug! It touched your heart and brain and your soul like a *hammer that pounded and pounded again!*

At first, people were not so addicted and could remove the head-piece. But later, after more and more of its usage, *you didn't take off the Id-Master.* People kept it on and it **consumed the body, heart and soul><.**

There were a very few people in the Electric State that realized who created the Id-Masters and who pushed them heavily on TV channels. (People had no cable TV, social media, personal phones, compact disks or computers). Yes, there was a small minority that saw the Tresen Corporation and the Id-devices for what they were: Dangerous. Deadly. And maybe the end of everything human? Nothing could make the rebels, the contraries, put on an Id-Master, no matter what. But these people had no voice or influence or power. No one could make changes. No one was permitted to discover anything significant or make a quantum leap for mankind. No one could change the face of the world. Humanity wallowed in a stagnant pool of crap.

A.I. Machine will not let us live up to our great potential. Crash of Worlds was not enough! The planet's depopulation from billions to thousands was not enough! Global A.I. had to destroy what IT thought were the last traces of freedom and free-thought! The last people. The Machine, and only the Machine, assumed ultimate control after 5/1/84...*because everything from then on was not real.*

Now the Machine will make reality loop again, as it did before...

Author's Comments on the 10 Stories:

1) The Phantom of the Broadway Show.

Remember Phantom of the Opera? Which one? There was Lon Chaney's silent version that contained one of the most horrific scenes ever filmed at the time, when the girl ripped the mask off of the Phantom. That face scared a lot of people. Then there was the 1962 Hammer version in bloody technicolor that I remember with Herbert Lom as Erik, the Phantom. But it's Michael Crawford's portrayal of the Phantom that people most remember. He gave 1300 performances over a 3½-year period and won a Tony Award. His performance was described as "haunting, sinister, and sensual."

I had to invent a Broadway play. Why not: *Dogs?* Of course, to parody *Cats*. Maybe the toughest part was writing a few lyrics of a Broadway-type showtune. Not my type of music. I casted Carol Lynley in the female lead because I happened to see a bit of her in an old movie and she could sing. The plot was clear in my mind although I was 11 when I saw the movie. The Phantom was an unknown who actually wrote a potential hit Opera, and it was stolen by a famous playwright. They fought and the unknown writer was burned in a fire. In my version, a famous playwright stole a potential hit Broadway show. How? It was easy to come up with: The unknown man simply did not register the play, and the famous man was within his rights to claim it as his. The scene of a split curtain and a dead man who swung out over the stage was taken directly from the Hammer film. I liked the idea it was a guy in a cat-suit, as if a crazy dog just didn't like cats. Cocaine, and being a secret transgender, certainly fueled the madness of the famous man and critic.

I usually write and write a story, then "rush to the end." Or, "cut to the chase." I want to end it fast after a considerable build-up. In this case, how to end it swiftly? Ah, a hidden camera in Amandiss' dressing room where he confessed that he did not write Dogs, that he was the murderer and revealed what he really was.

Showtunes and Broadway are far from my world; I'm more comfortable on Alpha Centauri with the Orions. Anyway, I liked it.

2) Sky Captain and the World Beyond.

This short story was such a joy to write because I am in love with the movie *Sky Captain and the World of Tomorrow*. I saw it a few times in the theater. I had it on disk and watched it often. The CGI imagery for every background scene was marvelous – the computers visualized anything while actors acted in front of green screens. The numbered, giant walkers were taken right out of Max Fleicher's animated Superman (1941-1943). My "Rocketeers" and "Bulleteers" were also taken from the old, animated, Superman series. The flying crafts, the buildings, the colors and the LOOK of everything in 'Captain' was in that old-fashioned art deco-style. I loved its cinematography. I loved what this CGI tool of imagination produced for our eyes. I'm sorry I didn't do a "lens cap" joke. *Sky Captain* is one of my favorite movies! Where's the sequel?

I'm not sure exactly what 'Sky Captain and the World Beyond' is, but I found two fantastic images as if there was a sequel. Then, I take these stories or mixtures or twists of stories and think: *Can I write a sequel? Or come up with an interesting twist to a classic? Or mix two independent stories and make them connect?* These are challenges for me. A small idea can spark a lengthy story.

I wanted desperately to do a Sky Captain story, only it had to be big! He wasn't Sky Captain; he was *Space Captain!* As it turned out, there were two of them. Two Dexs, and one was an enhanced Dex, more like an alien.

I had used the Norcatava machine before (the novel: 'Tera'). It brought fictional, fantasy-stuff from films, *into the real world.* I thought of using it in reverse: The Atavacron from Star Trek where real people basically lost themselves and lived forever as TV or movie characters. No one could stop **The Nothing**, the oncoming DOOM/DARKNESS that will destroy everything!! But they could hide from it and seal themselves in fictional scenarios, programs. I thought the character-choices the main characters chose were funny.

One more time, the story writes itself while I am writing it. I had the new title of 'World Beyond' from the very beginning. But I had no clue that the plot that forms in front of me would in any way tie into "World Beyond" …and it did. Totenkopf didn't make it in the sequel.

3) **Panday.**

Panday was a strange one to write. I don't know what I originally was thinking to come up with 'Pan,' and searched for *Pan…*

But I came across pictures of, apparently, something that is huge in China. I sure haven't seen the movies; maybe I'll look for them? I read very little of the Panday story and chose to make one up on my own. It's simply from observing the picture or pictures and then letting my mind Fly Free: What do these images do for me? Where do they take me? And, *voila,* the story just comes into focus very quickly.

Why not have a valiant, brave story that we've seen a hundred times before from Spartacus, to Moses, to Sidhartha, to the Thief of Bagdad, to Jesus? A poor man leads a group of rebels and it turns into a massive movement of people against an evil empire. A story of war and a fight for freedom and glory so oppressed people are no longer enslaved.

Sounds good. But is it, if the film franchise mutated over time and became *continuous blood and guts?* If it was nothing but VIOLENCE and bloodbaths and had lost its positive message over the course of sequels? Then you got children with swords involved, as if violence was the way to solve disputes?

I turned the story sideways when I brought in the Mandela Effect. The fictional Panday story had an evil emperor who made a mandatory Kill-Day or Purge-Day called "Pan." It was an 8th day to the week. Well, maybe, Panday-mania grew to such a global extent that Reality itself Shifted? Now, there was a Panday in the real world! *You could kill anyone and anyone could kill you.* It was suddenly a reality around you once every 8 days! The movie mandate seeped into the physical world and threatened everyone's lives. If anyone checked into it, they discovered we've had Panday for years and years! What? Since when? It's the new reality everyone must live and die with.

What made the end of the Panday story effective was the 8 Day a Week, monthly calendar. It was not difficult to change a normal calendar into a Panday calendar. Pandays were marked in red.

It was a horrendous warning of the insanity of mob-mentality, a statement against fascism and how we should be free to think independently~.

4) **Willy Tonka.**

Willy Tonka is the gem in Storybook 5. It began with a single photo-find of a real, yellow, full-size Truck with "Tonka" and "T-Rex" written on it. I immediately made the joke, "Willy Tonka" and that's all I needed. What would the movie have been like if it wasn't Wonka, a chocolate bar, but Tonka, a truck you drive on the road?

I start at the beginning and go from there. The film is so well-known to Baby-Boomers, such a classic. Willy Tonka's hat, jacket, Loompa Oompas and most of the things in Tonkaland were yellow. It was because of the fine photo I found of a Tonka yellow truck.

I refreshed myself on parts of the original movie on a movie channel. Only certain parts, to get the lyrics of the songs and some of the dialog exactly. Much of the story was indelibly etched in my brain. I created a Snide character, which paralleled Slugworth in the movie. When I saw the part with this odd character, I was surprised: I pictured a whole other actor, tall, in black/top hat, bald. When I saw Slugworth, he was a completely different guy than I imagined.

I created a *Jennifer Seether* character and only real deep students of my work will figure out why. The reason is Veruca Salt was her name in the movie and a name of an '80s alternative music band. The band's one hit song was called: 'Seether.' There's an actress called Jennifer Salt. If you can put all those pieces together, then you are a Bonafide Brainiac!

Once again, I just write/write/write and lo and behold, all the parts come together like silk…in a way I certainly had not planned. I sure took the basic elements in the movie (don't know about the book) and wrote my version of most of them. I'm very proud of this one. Less than two days of work!

I am so excited that I am sending a hardcopy of *Willy Tonka* to the Chairman of the Hasbro Company! Hasbro bought Tonka years ago. My idea is: I want to do for Hasbro/Tonka what Transformers did for Mattel. I want to do what filmmakers have done with Legos. There are no Tonka movies. Maybe we only need a good script? I think it's a slam-dunk winner and would love to see a movie with this quote in the credits: "Based on a short story by TS Caladan." Maybe one day?

5) **Moon Oblivion.**

Okay. I am also very proud of 'Moon Oblivion' and how it turned out. The story changed again and again while I wrote it. To appreciate what I've done, you have to be familiar with the 2 movies I combined: *Moon,* with Sam Rockwell, and *Oblivion,* with Tom Cruise.

I wasn't sure exactly how to do it, because I get these movies confused; they are very similar. But once I saw the movie poster for *Oblivion* and saw that I could make "Moon" out of the "Oblivion" letters, I was excited. I didn't know how I would merge the movies, as yet, but I knew that I could – and it would be good – and this was all because I made a movie poster called: <u>Moon Oblivion</u>. Combination of the titles amazed me because: They made sense and were a part of the film's plot, the destruction of the Moon.

My story in its entirety is complex and both movie elements blend into one at certain points. The idea was the Tom Cruise clones in the beginning changed into the other film and it was still Cruise because he was in a spacesuit. His name wasn't Jack Harper, as it was in *Oblivion*...I kept it "Sam Bell," that was Sam Rockwell's name or name of the clones' original in *Moon*. Even his wife, Tess Bell, was used and that went back to Moon and not the Oblivion story.

Morgan Freeman's character in Oblivion was Malcolm Beech. I changed it to Brighton Beech. There's a Brighton Beach in England.

The plot in Oblivion was a clever mind-bender and so was the plot in Moon once you realized what was going on. The Company (as in 'Alien') or the Corporation or the A.I. Drones in Oblivion, they're the bad-guys. It wasn't difficult to extrapolate it all into a familiar "War with the Machines," like *Matrix* or *Terminator*.

My first storylines I thought were going to be about a computer that desired very much to not be only a digital entity, but a humanoid that walked and talked and even felt sensations. It worked hard to lift itself out of the system. A machine that became human. But that concept I saved for the end of the story where Sam met the computer, Gertie (from *Moon*), face-to-face on a Moon with an atmosphere. There were a lot of pictures in this "movie" of mine and they completely determined the story, once I strung it all together.

For sure, one of my favorite combinations of stories.

6) **Czardoz.**

Zardoz was an interesting movie to me. Possibly the execution of it could have been better. Fascinating concept: To build a world where people could not die. In that futuristic society, people's minds would develop powers eventually, psychic powers, powers of telekinesis where you moved objects with your brain. A look could hurt or many looks could kill. Criminals were aged, so that they had to go through eternity as old men and old women who never died. If something deadly happened to you, the Tabernacle rebuilt you to the age you were.

People were tired with life, tired of living, after so much time. That was the interesting part. After living hundreds and hundreds of years, they were bored with life. Sick of it and very much desired death! That's what Zed (Sean Connery) brought to the psi-community. Him and his men slaughtered the "Eternals." After The Crystal was 'destroyed,' the Tabernacle was ruined; no one was rebuilt and Death came to an immortal society.

My version had a small group of very old scientists who weren't exterminated. They truly wanted to live. They built small robots who constructed larger robots. A new modern age began again with the completion of Tabernacle II. Their goal was to repopulate the Earth. They did, with a refurbished Crystal. Everything was wonderful for the longest time.

Alpha (Zed) was the first man created in the New Order and new age for humanity. Sara (Consuella), his mate, was the first woman. They became King and Queen. He is called the "Czar" and started out as a good, kind King. But power corrupts; he fights with his Queen and I don't have an ending yet, at the time of this writing, but I will.

Once again, like *Willy Tonka,* I came up with "Czardoz" first, but I knew nothing of the story at the time. I knew I could use the title and imagine a plot to go with it. Then I saw the poster and changed the top line: Instead of Zed bringing Death to a world of Life, I reversed it where he'll bring Life to a world of Death.

Correction: I don't know how the later Czardoz story will flow, but I do know the very last line. I had the final joke early on. That Janus, the oldest one, would say: "Maybe we shouldn't live forever?"

7) **Dayfall.**

Once more, readers have to be familiar with Isaac Asimov's 'Nightfall' to fully understand my completely opposite story. To me, *Nightfall* is one of the greatest short stories ever written! [Asimov trying to be a physicist and astronomer. Wonder who really wrote the classics? Certainly, not the "names" that are credited with the stories].

"**Nightfall**"[1] is a 1941 science-fiction short story by the American writer Isaac Asimov about the coming of darkness to the people of a planet ordinarily illuminated by sunlight at all times. It was adapted into a novel with Robert Silverberg in 1990. The short story has appeared in many anthologies and six collections of Asimov stories. In 1968, the Science Fiction Writers of America voted "Nightfall" the best science fiction short story written prior to the 1965 establishment of the Nebula Awards and included it in *The Science Fiction Hall of Fame, Volume One, 1929–1964*.

What an incredible concept that somewhere in the universe could actually happen: People on a planet with multiple suns *never experienced night!* Except, once every millennium when all the suns were aligned perfectly straight in their orbits, then a large/dark planet eclipsed them all! This caused **NIGHT**! For the first time in their lives and for ages, the Great Cycle repeated, and Night fell upon the world and the world experienced total Darkness! What would happen?

Asimov's tale said the people went mad. Wouldn't you, if you never experienced night? You'd know shadows and semi-darkness, but never the pitch black of Night. They couldn't imagine *the Stars* and what a night's sky appeared like. People on the planet had very old legends of the darkness and the madness and destruction that went with it. Fires were lit for light, and their world burned. Fear of the unknown, Fear of the Dark, destroyed their simple and superstitious society when Night fell. It occurred regularly, every millennium.

I had to twist it all around and describe an opposite situation. These aliens only knew and experienced The Dark. They had no clue what light was or what their kind was or what their world looked like. They felt everything; they heard everything, but they saw only BLACKNESS. Then a very rare, astronomical situation happened and LIGHT appeared for the first time in their lives! Light! That showed the aliens what they truly looked like and what their environment truly appeared like. What would happen when the creatures saw the light?

8) **Gung Fu.**

Here's a hilarious story and a lot of it is true. The Twist isn't. It is a pure fact that many do not know:

Bruce Lee created the Kung Fu TV series, and that series was *one of the greatest, ever!* Kung Fu had excellent ratings and was up there with Star Trek and The Twilight Zone. Thoughtful, eastern philosophies that were dispensed between (slow-motion) action scenes were wonderful and very memorable. American living rooms should have been honored to have been given Shaolin temple wisdom. Sadly, many of the beautiful life-lessons flew over most people's heads. Kung Fu aired for 3 seasons and 62 episodes. The narrative is: "The series ended because David Carradine wanted to pursue a movie career and he kept getting hurt." Odd, because he hardly did anything in Kung Fu's *fight* scenes.

Yes, everything about Kung Fu originated from the mind of Bruce Lee. He was cheated, given a hard time and not cast as Caine – yet the "suits" went ahead with his show and gave the lead role to someone else? What!? And the part was given to a known alcoholic, trouble-maker and a Legacy (John's son). I changed his name to "Karradine" since I was sure to sling some "trash" his way, to oppose a real hero: Bruce Lee.

I believe Bruce was PUNISHED when they stole Kung Fu from him and maybe "forced" him into the role of Kato, Green Hornet's driver. What a turnabout! Everyone knows how amazing Kato's martial arts moves were on 'Hornet,' and how awful the action was by Carradine in 'Kung Fu.' *They had to use slow-motion,* as we know.

I twisted it, and…My way is how it should have gone down: Lee plays Caine (as he should have) and let's punish Carradine (or Karradine) and have him play Kato on a cheesy TV show. Perfect. That's how I drew it up.

Also, I hinted that Bruce Lee was *murdered* because

he was going to "spill the beans" and expose corruption in the movie industry. Was he murdered because he was a rebel and "didn't play ball" with the masters above his level, the people who made him? Did they also kill his son, Brandon? Who knows?

No photo of Carradine in a Kato outfit, but I did find a late photo of him in a limo – and I said it was the Hornet's Black Beauty. Ha.

9) **Battlestar Atlantica.**

I mentioned "deep students of my work." *If I only had some* – this is the story to analyze, study and investigate further. Sure, it is an obvious parody of TV's 'Battlestar Galactica.' In fact, in the original pilot episode, which showed the destruction of Caprica by Cylons, might have had a Battlestar named "Atlantis," if memory serves. This is not a story about one of those type of Battlestars and a ragtag team of survivors that followed along out into space.

It's similar, but twisted to conform to Genesis theories of mine that I have studied and developed ever since 1974! What if the big secret that very few people realize is: *We are Martians!* We are the Martians and Mars had beautiful, Earth-like conditions 60,000 years ago! Mars was ruined, turned red by radiation (I believe) because of an event, namely the *destruction of the 5th planet, which created the Asteroid Belt.* And human refugees fled a decimated world, made it to Earth and started the colony of Atlantis 60,000 years ago.

I turned the TV show around: It was the destruction of Atlantis on Earth! Machines eventually got out of control after a long-standing Paradise and planned a takeover~. They created Cylons: Machine forces that blew up the global Grid and left Earth powerless, killed millions and the few that remained were helpless and defenseless! One of the Security saucers or "Battlestars," armed with potent sniper-craft, launched and along with it were the last humans. Humans who searched space for their home world, from tens of thousands of years ago. All the navigation from the original migration was gone. Where was Caprica and what state would the Capricans be in if found?

These late Atlanteans discovered that *Mars was Caprica!* Home world wasn't many lightyears away, it was only a matter of millions of miles away, the next planet. Mars/Caprica was cleaned up from the ruins of a Super Utopia that once existed there. It remained red, but not toxic in any way. The planet was ripe for colonization.

Earthlings found that "Protectors," whatever they were, placed the Martian survivors (Indians) in a protective dome – knowing that their brothers (gods) in space would return and build a new Mars. They were camouflaged, so no alien, Cylon or human knew they existed. Humans began again on the same world they had started from<>.

10) What was said between Elvis and Dylan when they Fought in Dune 2?

I got such a kick out of this one when the lightning bolt struck me to do it. Austin Butler had played Elvis and Timothee Chalamet played Bob Dylan. In Dune 2, the actors had a fight scene. Maybe the microphones were off? Maybe they were told to mix it up and the best shots would be edited into the final version? Maybe no one heard them and sound-effects would be added in post-production?

The short piece was completed in only a few minutes. I made sure every box was checked on what I wanted to say. I think everything is there. I thought it was funny and revealing. Butler came along a little before Chalamet and knew a bit more of how the industry works and how to get on Hollywood's "gravy train."

I left it as a Surprise Story because it sure surprised me and quickly came out of thin air. I've heard people speak of the greatness of Elvis Presley and *I just have to laugh.* There are real talents in the world and one of them was not Elvis Presley. I've heard defenders of "the King" give the same arguments I included in the story. Tell me, do you think the *guy* was overrated and a product of hype?

Let's look at "the great" (not-so-great) Bob Dylan. I hope I've placed enough clues, breadcrumbs or bits of suspicion that might make readers *investigate.* Not typical Dylan information, but dirty – seedy underbelly-type material – and you could change your high opinion of Bob Dylan. **Hollywood never gives us the truth.**

Do we really know for sure that anyone wrote anything or truly were responsible for the songs or books they are credited for creating? No, we do not. Instead of people blindly believing what They tell us, maybe we should question what They tell us? Maybe we should research and dig a little deeper? Maybe we should be open to different ideas/different from what Media has always pushed down our throats?

How to end the 10th story? I'd touch base with the Bohemian Grove. Instead of saying, "I'll see you there,"

Butler gave Chalamet a warning that implied, in future, the boy will really be in for it by his masters. [Maybe the same group who ruled the life of Bruce Lee?]. And the "sacrifices" that are in store for you as you journey this path.

12) **The Electric State Loop.**

Simon Stalenhag's graphic novels called: 'Tales from the Loop' and 'The Electric State' are amazing and have thrilled viewers. They are more artbooks with a wild story attached to them than graphic novels. My theory (as with Dali, Moebius, etc.) is that the young man didn't paint his paintings – they are too well done – he is too prolific - they were created by committee: a talented group of international artists, then heavily pushed around the world by the secret masters of the world. Why would I believe such a thing?

Because people might be slowly waking up to the fact that CERN (Stalenhag's "Loop") might not be an atomic Collider? Its influence over decades may have produced a Clash of Worlds, universes? Why are so many movies and animated films suddenly about parallel worlds? Why is the world now very different from the way it was? The "Multi-verse" is a term often used these days. If you read Stalenhag's Picture-Books, you might realize "his" story actually explains what many have called the "Mandela Effect." (I've written 2 books about the phenomenon). *His Collider, the great Loop, caused a different past to emerge, one with strange machines frozen in time that littered the landscape.* He is Swedish, a location not far from CERN. He is an international "star and musician." And now, his artwork and stories have inspired a new movie called: 'The Electric State,' which stars Chris Pratt and Millie Bobby Brown. How does Stalenhag's art and stories get pushed in every country and made into movies? Because he's so incredibly talented? No. Because the committee's message to the world, like other movies, is a secret message to what THEY have done to every person and the whole planet: We have *reality-shifted* to the Dark Side…and a Machine did it.

It was not difficult for me to simplify the story and have the A.I. behind all the human genocide. Maybe the horrible, secret truth shouldn't be shoved in our face in the form of fictional movies and entertainment? Maybe we deserve better than that? I was so looking forward to watching *The Electric State* film, to see the amazing panels of artwork come to life on a big screen. Wouldn't you know it? The reviews of the movie were awful! Terrible! THEY just cannot give people today quality stories and music. Such a damn shame~~~.

Books written by TS Caladan (DH Jetson):

1) The Continuum
2) Son of Zog
3) The Cydonian War
4) Science-Faction [Vol. 1]
5) Science-Faction [Vol. 2]
6) ANAGRAMACRON
7) inspiration
8) 2099, Transia~
9) The New Men and the New World
10) Beyond Barronsland
11) Mandela Effect
12) Best of TS Caladan
13) Mandela Effect II
14) Collected Comedy of TS Caladan
15) TS Caladan's Comedy II
16) Pez Wars
17) The PEZ-Effect
18) Ceana
19) PEZ 4 Ever
20) My Cat Book
21) Artificial *Intelligense*
22) Teran Tales
23) Another Tera
24) Tera
25) 1001 Coincidences
26) Coincidences Continue*
27) 100 Very Short Stories
28) The Krown of Power
29) More Short Stories
30) Storybook Three
31) IF – Storybook Four
32) Long Short Stories – Storybook 5

TS Caladan

Dedicated to the Survivors...
in the Next World

TS Caladan

Doug was born the only son of Rose and Steve Yurchey in Bridgeville, PA. in 1951. A loner, he drew pictures and dreamed of big/bright, colorful, fantasy-worlds that were inside the comic book adventures he cherished. Movies, TV, stories, art, thrilled the young man, especially sci-fi and anything that had to do with aliens and life on other planets. He grew up interested in sports and earned a half-scholarship in tennis to Edinboro State. After college, his interests turned to astronomy and various mysteries.

An unexpected event occurred: In 1973, he fell in love with a psychic who channeled. A three and a half-year marriage and a 'virtual Close Encounter' later, the young man was motivated to discover the truth in everything<. Odd occurrences happened during a strange marriage where spoons and keys bent with the powers of the mind. They met mentalist Uri Geller at this time. Wife Katrina did similar telepathic and "spoon bending" feats and their closest friends witnessed extraordinary things. In late 1977, the marriage ended.

Doug moved to LA in 1982. He worked on the Simpsons Show in 1990-1991 as a background "Clean-

Up" artist. After 2000, he became a prolific writer with many online articles, radio interviews and YouTubes of his work on Atlantis, Nikola Tesla and the ancient World Grid. He was on 'Coast-to-Coast with George Noory' radio show and gave "the best interview since John Lear." Doug was filmed by National Geographic filmmaker Diego D'Innocenzo because of his theories on the prehistoric, rust-less, Iron Pillar in New Delhi. Nine million Italians saw the production on a TV Science show called 'Voyager,' with special-effects.

His writing dreams came true and he was published by TWB Press in 2015. Now '*TS Caladan,*' the author's interests are Modern Mysteries and conspiracies or secrets behind Hollywood and the Illuminati. Then he discovered the Mandela Effect in 2019, which *changed everything~*. Tray Caladan is a mystery himself. He has spent more than 50 years of pure, honest, scientific research and today uses artwork and wild/far-out, sci-fi stories to deliver his conclusions and positive messages...*and, still, no one believes him.* [A few do].

TS Caladan

Contact information for Tray Samuel Caladan:

tscaladan@gmail.com

Questions and comments are very welcome. Readers will receive quick replies. Thank you very much.

~tsc

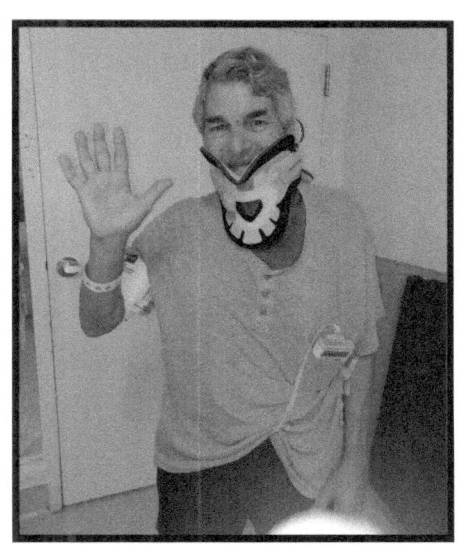

https://www.twbpress.com
Science Fiction – Supernatural – Horror – Thriller
and more